"You do like me. And I think you want me as much as I want you."

He didn't say anything more. He didn't do anything more.

This was it? He was telling her to go to sleep right after making her think that he was about to seduce her right here and now?

"Princes," she murmured against his collarbone as she tucked her head under his chin. "You can't make them see reason, you can't shoot them."

A low chuckle shook him.

Oh, that he had the gall to laugh at her. "Once we get out of these godforsaken catacombs, I hope never to see you again, Your Highness." She added the formality at the end to drive the point home.

"I suppose you could keep your eyes closed, but it won't be much fun."

Her head came up, but she couldn't make out the expression on his face. "What are you talking about?"

His arms tightened around her. "As soon as we get out of here, I'm planning on making love to you, madam."

DANA MARTON

ROYAL PROTOCOL

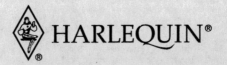

HARLEQUIN®

TORONTO • NEW YORK • LONDON
AMSTERDAM • PARIS • SYDNEY • HAMBURG
STOCKHOLM • ATHENS • TOKYO • MILAN • MADRID
PRAGUE • WARSAW • BUDAPEST • AUCKLAND

To Denise Zaza and Allison Lyons. Thank you again!

Recycling programs
for this product may
not exist in your area.

ISBN-13: 978-0-373-88916-7

ROYAL PROTOCOL

Copyright © 2009 by Dana Marton

www.eHarlequin.com

Printed in U.S.A.

ABOUT THE AUTHOR

Dana Marton is the author of more than a dozen fast-paced, action-adventure romantic suspense novels and a winner of the Daphne du Maurier Award of Excellence. She loves writing books of international intrigue, filled with dangerous plots that try her tough-as-nails heroes and the special women they fall in love with. Her books have been published in seven languages in eleven countries around the world. When not writing or reading, she loves to browse antique shops and enjoys working in her sizable flower garden where she searches for "bad" bugs with the skills of a superspy and vanquishes them with the agility of a commando soldier. Every day in her garden is a thriller. To find more information on her books, please visit www.danamarton.com. She would love to hear from her readers and can be reached via e-mail at the following address: DanaMarton@DanaMarton.com.

Books by Dana Marton

HARLEQUIN INTRIGUE
806—SHADOW SOLDIER
821—SECRET SOLDIER
859—THE SHEIK'S SAFETY
875—CAMOUFLAGE HEART
902—ROGUE SOLDIER
917—PROTECTIVE
      MEASURES
933—BRIDAL OP
962—UNDERCOVER SHEIK
985—SECRET CONTRACT*
991—IRONCLAD COVER*
1007—MY BODYGUARD*

1013—INTIMATE DETAILS*
1039—SHEIK SEDUCTION
1055—72 HOURS
1085—SHEIK PROTECTOR
1105—TALL, DARK AND LETHAL
1121—DESERT ICE DADDY
1136—SAVED BY THE
      MONARCH†
1142—ROYAL PROTOCOL†

*Mission: Redemption
†Defending the Crown

CAST OF CHARACTERS

Prince Benedek Kerkay—The youngest prince bucked protocol before, with tragic consequences, and has since sworn to follow the royal directive. But when his world is threatened by rebels, will he give up the one woman he loves but can never have?

Rayne Williams—An opera singing sensation, she has her protective walls safely in place. But one young prince threatens to bring down those walls even as he saves her from the rebels. Or is he the real danger?

Chancellor Egon—The new chancellor's obsession is to see all the princes married off according to protocol. If they let him.

Vilmos—A royal guard whose only objective should be to keep the monarchy safe. But is he ruled by his past?

Arpad Kerkay—The crown prince is a colonel in the air force. Since the queen is ill, soon he will inherit the crown.

Miklos Kerkay—Second to the throne. He is an army major and a happily married man.

Janos Kerkay—Third in line to the throne. He is an economist, as well as a superb yachtsman who also regularly wins golf championships.

Istvan Kerkay—Fourth in line to the throne. He is a cultural anthropologist who is obsessed with preserving the past of his country. He's somewhat of an introvert, but speaks a dozen languages fluently.

Lazlo Kerkay—(Benedek's twin) Fifth in line to the throne. Lazlo is a successful entrepreneur whose company builds race cars. He is also an avid racer, somewhat of a gambler and the ladies' man in the family.

Chapter One

Benedek Kerkay, youngest prince of Valtria, stared at the evenly printed lines on the paper, but all he could see was the face of the most beautiful woman in the universe, the one who'd been holding him enthralled for years. A woman he could never have.

"Protesters are gathering at Liberation Square, Your Highness." His secretary stood in the door of his temporary office at the Royal Opera House, shifting from one scrawny leg to the other.

Benedek cleared his head and processed the man's words, forgetting the speech he should have been rehearsing for the reopening of the three-hundred-year-old opera house, his most significant project yet as an architect. His muscles drew tight. "No. Absolutely not."

Morin looked gravely ahead. A peculiar-looking little man, he was loyal to the bone at a time when loyalty was scarce. For this, he was much appreciated at the palace. He'd been with the House of Kerkay since Benedek could remember, even forsaking family for service, although rumors about him and the head housekeeper of the palace's east wing circulated from time to time. He was such a private man that even Benedek didn't know the truth of those rumors. Nor was he in the mood to speculate on them at the moment.

"There can't be a protest tonight." He came out of his seat and strode to the exquisitely restored six-foot-tall window, turning his back to Morin, wishing he could see across the five-acre Millennial Park to Liberation Square.

His fists tightened, crushing the sheets he held. Nothing would be allowed to upset the peace tonight. He'd been working toward this night for the last five years, restoring the Baroque-style building with painstaking care. Close to a thousand nobles, Valtrian celebrities and foreign dignitaries were invited to the opening night and were even now taking their seats. Rayne Williams, opera diva, "the voice of the night," was giving her first performance outside of the U.S. in a decade.

"Call in Royal Security, call in the army, call in the National Guard, call in the synchronized parachuters for all I care, but do *not*—" he relaxed his clenched jaw muscles "—let anyone spoil tonight."

"Yes, Your Highness. Only that it's—" His secretary hesitated.

Benedek crushed the papers tighter, knowing from the look on the man's face that he wasn't going to like what he was about to hear. "Only what?"

"A show of force at the present moment— against peaceful protesters."

Benedek walked to his desk then back to the window, pacing the antique reproduction carpet. Disbanding the protesters by force could look like an attempt to silence the voice of the people. Not a year after the siege of Maltmore Castle where the enemies of the monarchy had attempted to kill the entire royal family and take over the country, where dozens of people died in a night of bloodshed... The royal guard marching on the people might not be the smartest thing politically. The country needed reconciliation and joint steps toward unity.

He hated politics. He'd become an architect partially for that reason. Buildings were simple. Buildings were stable. Buildings didn't stab you in the back.

"Who's handling it?"

"The police, Your Highness. Your brother Miklos is keeping a close eye on it as well."

Miklos was an Army major. He had an interest in security and also played a role in it. "Call the chief of palace security and tell him I need to talk to him. Here." Benedek was escorting Rayne to a reception at the palace after her performance. Palace Hill was just a few blocks away, not that far from Liberation Square. He needed to discuss these new developments with the chief. Maybe they needed to alter their plans. "I want the protest carefully watched and every change reported." He drew a slow breath, nodded beyond his office door. "Are they ready?"

"Yes, Your Highness."

He tossed his crumpled speech on his desk, on top of a stack of blueprints and photos of the various stages of the building's restoration. This building meant everything to him. His oldest brother, Arpad, had ribbed him about wanting to show the country that he was more than the youngest prince at the palace. Maybe there was some truth in that, but the project was more. It was his validation as an architect.

He straightened his tuxedo jacket. "How do I look?"

Morin seemed surprised by the question.

And Benedek was instantly annoyed that he'd asked. On any other day, he would have been too busy drawing blueprints in his mind to pay much attention to his appearance.

"Splendid, Your Highness," Morin said at last, after an awkward silence.

Benedek nodded his thanks, knowing the compliment meant little. As a prince he was used to hearing what everyone thought he wanted to hear.

Except when it came to bloody protesters.

He passed by his secretary, strode down the hallway that looked majestic even in the staff areas where the audience would never wander. He waved his new bodyguard away. "Wait for me at the royal box," he told the man, turning down the hall. He missed his old guard who had recently retired. He hadn't had a chance to develop the same kind of rapport with this one yet. And he didn't need anyone hovering at his back when he finally met Rayne Williams.

The rich carpet softened his steps on the antique floorboards. The building was like a grande dame of old with gracious curves and resplendent gilding, tantalizing textures and colors. He didn't stop until he reached the door at the very end. The sign on the door simply said *Rayne.* He adjusted his tie one last time then knocked.

"Come in."

He pushed the door wide with a smile, then stopped midmotion to stare. An unprincely thing to do. He needed to stop reacting to her like a moon-eyed teenager.

He'd seen her perform in New York several times, but Rayne Williams was a thousand times more beautiful up close. Silver eyes shone out of a face that was perfectly symmetrical; her skin was translucent and glowing, her lips ruby-glossed. Ebony strands of silky hair cascaded to well below her slim waist, while more was piled intricately at the back of her head. She was willowy, although not as tall as he was, wearing a burgundy gown, the copy of one worn by a historical heroine of Valtria at her royal wedding. The corset pushed up her breasts to the point of nearly spilling from the brocade, as had been the custom of that age.

He was all for historical accuracy. Absolutely.

He bowed deeply before she could notice his rapt attention to her cleavage. "Welcome to Valtria."

"Thank you, Prince Benedek. I understand you'll be escorting me to the stage tonight."

She was unfailingly polite, even though she disliked him. He knew that for a fact. But her voice, soft and rich, still had the power to keep him spellbound. He was to be her escort for tonight. Not nearly enough, although he'd come to accept that her remote behavior toward him was for the best.

For years, he'd gone to her performances in the U.S., sometimes two or three times a year, sending her a bouquet of Valtria's signature purple roses each time, always with an invitation to dinner. Her response notes were always the same, she felt honored but no thanks.

And no matter how much he wanted to get

closer to her, he'd never pushed beyond that. Because even as he'd fantasized about taking her as a lover, he was afraid that might not be enough. His twin brother, Lazlo, was the consummate ladies' man. Benedek was more of a one-woman kind of guy. And Rayne Williams could never be his one woman.

He could never have her forever. He could absolutely not marry an American singer, no matter how famous and respected. The scandal alone would kill his ailing mother. Dark memories surfaced. He pushed them back. He wouldn't make a mistake of that magnitude again. He was a prince. He was to marry a daughter of the Valtrian nobility who was even now being selected behind closed doors by the chancellor and his team.

Seeing how much positive publicity Miklos's marriage and the birth of his son had brought to the monarchy, the new chancellor was obsessed with marrying off the rest of the princes. And Benedek was determined not to buck protocol again. He'd done that before with disastrous consequences.

He cleared his throat, then did his best to clear his mind of all the things he and Miss Williams could be doing instead of walking to the stage. He was a grown man, thirty two years old. He'd had lovers, passion, disappointments. Tragedies.

But Rayne Williams was Rayne Williams.

"If you will allow me the honor, Madam," he said and offered his arm.

After tonight, she would stay for three more days in Valtria. Three days in which he would content himself with admiring her from afar and would not, under any circumstances, seduce her. Not that she looked like she would let him if he tried. Still the challenge— He killed that thought without mercy and took in those silver eyes that held nothing but politeness. No batting of the lashes, none of the come-hither looks he was used to from women.

On this count, at least, the royal family seemed safe from trouble.

TROUBLE WITH A ROYAL TITLE—Rayne summed up the man in front of her and continued wearing her stage smile.

He was as handsome as the devil himself, a prince spoiled by privilege, and way too young to be looking at her the way he had from the moment he'd set foot inside her dressing room.

If he noted the conspicuous lack of a gushing response to the enormous bouquet of purple roses he'd sent earlier, he didn't show it. The roses, like all other flowers she received, were usually distributed among the support staff.

He was an exceedingly charismatic man in person, she noted with dismay. She'd been right to stay away from him. He carried himself with the unconscious grace of nobility, his body toned and agile. From what she'd read, all the Valtrian princes were serious sportsmen, and it certainly showed. The youngest prince of Valtria was no palace weakling; he was built tough like most of his countrymen. She supposed it came from living in this rugged country at the foot of the Alps.

"Whenever you're ready." He smiled a charmer's smile. It looked unfairly good on him.

And despite her misgivings, she placed her hand onto his offered arm. She was taken by surprise when a shock wave of connection and awareness shot all the way to her elbow, despite the barrier of his tuxedo and her satin gloves between them.

She caught her breath, but said, "Let's go

then." And glided alongside him without the slightest pause. She was a professional performer. If she didn't want him to know the effect he had on her then, by God, he wouldn't.

She'd been pursued by enough presumptuous rich men who thought all performers were of loose morals, living only to be pretty and to satisfy their every desire. They sent flowers to her dressing room, truffles, even jewelry. They had their expensive cars wait for her at the actors' exit after performances. She'd always sent the chauffeurs home with an empty backseat.

Leaders of industry, even public figures showed up in her dressing room, ready for a quick tumble, treating her like she was the flavor of the month out of some musical revue at a downtown theatre. They didn't know anything about her, nothing at all.

She wasn't for sale, not ever again. All the rich perverts could keep their money and drown in it.

At forty, she was an accomplished singer and a woman of independent means. And she was damn proud of that.

But she did give a gracious smile to the handsome prince, even if she had the distinct feeling that she was being served on a silver platter to the man. To be invited to the re-opening of the Valtrian opera, a historic occasion, was an honor, regardless of the fact that she didn't want to be here. She would have rather chosen a place much closer to her home for her first transatlantic flight in a decade.

"Your tie is crooked," she told him, registering the fact automatically.

He would give her introduction. She didn't want him to go up on stage with his tie askew and have the audience looking at that instead of what he was doing. Checking and re-checking herself and the rest of the cast before shows was something she did without conscious thought.

An odd look flashed across his eyes as he reached up, his long, masculine fingers fumbling. Without a mirror, he had no idea what to adjust.

She drew a breath. "Let me." She was tall, but he was taller so she had to reach up. She straightened the black cloth at his neck, pulling back too fast when her knuckles brushed against his strong jawline for a second.

"Thank you, Madam." His focus on her never wavered.

Those intense dark eyes could be the doom of a woman if she weren't careful, she thought for a fanciful second before she gathered herself. She wasn't about to let on that she was oddly flustered. *Flustered.* At her age. By some prince nearly a decade her junior. How crazy was that? "Rayne, please, Your Highness." Everybody in the business called her Rayne.

"If you call me Benedek." His focused, mesmerizing intensity relaxed by a small degree.

He seemed pleased. Then he let go all the way, and the smile that slowly bloomed on his handsome face was absolutely stunning: warm, sexy, masculine. His eyes were the deep rich brown of the Swiss truffles she rewarded herself with on occasion. The manufacturer spoiled her with regular gifts, one of the perks of being a diva of her time. The title came with both advantages and disadvantages.

As did his, the thought crossed her mind. Maybe his life was as strange and as out of his hands at times as her own. Maybe they had something in common, after all.

His smile held. God help any unsuspecting woman he set his sights on. She was relieved to know that in three days, she would be leaving Valtria.

It'd been a long time since she'd been this aware of a man. She'd seen him before, but always from the stage, from a fair distance, even if he did sit in the best box each and every time. But now, having him this close and touching her, a faint charge ran along her skin, and she couldn't quite tell if it was a quick thrill or a shiver of foreboding.

She had little time to ponder it. The closer they got to the stage, the more energy filled her body. Yet, at the same time, a great calm descended on her mind. She was in the zone. She was doing what she loved. Singing was who she was. She could certainly ignore the bedroom eyes of a young European prince.

"It's too fuzzy! Who touched the ERS? Everything worked fine this morning, damn it." A little man rushed by, shouting to someone over his headset, demanding perfect stage lighting.

She didn't let that worry her. By the time the curtains rolled back, everything would be ready. She would focus only on her own performance. She'd learned that to pay attention to anyone else's was the surest way to get distracted.

People were scurrying about with small props and sheets of paper, losing their heads over some minor crisis or the other that tended to pop up before every show. Rayne focused on what she needed to do and routinely ignored the rest.

When they reached the steps that led up to the stage, the prince motioned her forward. In her mind, she was already singing the selection from Valtria's most famous operas. Troublesome princes with bedroom eyes or not, the country had had some brilliant composers.

She was on the second step when the building shook and she lost her footing in the period shoes that had been made to match her costume. She found herself, confused and alarmed, in the prince's arms. He'd been coming up behind her and had caught her when she'd stumbled.

His strong arms held her as if she were a precious treasure.

Protective.

She blinked the temporary fancy away. Over the years, a great many men had wanted to do a great many things with her. Protecting her had never been one of them.

"What was that?" she asked as he set her on her feet.

"This way." He grabbed her hand and dragged her back toward the dressing room with a dark expression on his face that stood in contrast to his seemingly pleased mood of before.

They met with his secretary halfway down the corridor, a man named Morin. She'd been introduced to him upon arrival. He was as skinny a man as she'd ever seen, with a rather large head and an incredibly long, thin nose. He kept his spine studiously straight and his shoulders pushed back. The first time she'd seen him, she'd thought he had an uncanny resemblance to a mosquito.

The image was reinforced now as, filled with nervous energy, he buzzed around the prince.

"The protest turned violent, Your Highness. A catering van just exploded in front of the opera house. There seems to be some confusion over whether it was an accident or intentional."

Her pulse quickened. "There's a protest?"

She hadn't turned on her television set in her hotel room since she'd arrived. She preferred to relax in silence when not practicing for her performance.

"Supposedly peaceful. I apologize," the prince said, keeping pace. "Order will be restored at any moment. We will delay the performance by just a few minutes." He fell silent for a beat. "No. An hour. In an hour I'll have this fully investigated."

A man in a dark suit came flying down the hall. "Everything all right, Your Highness?" He scanned their surroundings.

He looked like a bodyguard. Probably the prince's.

"You'll go with Miss Williams," Benedek told him.

The man looked decidedly uncomfortable as he fell in step with them. "I'm sorry, Your Highness, but I cannot do that." He looked extremely apologetic, but even more in-flexible on that issue. "I'm required—"

"Fine," Benedek cut him off and stopped at the point where the corridor came to a T. He turned to his secretary who'd been flitting along, wringing his hands. "Is the chief of palace security here?"

"On his way, Your Highness. I talked to him just a moment ago and—"

"I'm trusting you two to escort Miss Williams to the palace. Call for an armored car and as many royal guards as they can spare."

The man about snapped his heels together. "Certainly, Your Highness."

She hadn't been to the palace yet, although she was supposed to attend a reception there tonight. She didn't fancy going out to the streets just now. The opera house was giant and newly restored, looking sturdy enough to withstand a full-blown military attack if necessary.

"I'd prefer not to leave the building this close to my performance," she objected, but the prince seemed to be focused on something else and was already rushing off with a last, unfathomable look at her, his bodyguard in his wake, following closely.

"This way." Morin was certainly determined to obey his boss. He dialed his cell phone, his lips tightening. "The line's busy. He might be outside already, investigating the explosion."

She assumed he was talking about the chief of palace security.

Morin called for an armored car next. "We'll go out the back entrance," he said as he hung up.

She barely had time to process that before they neared the back door normally used by stage staff, where people were rushing out, then rushing right back in.

The secretary cast her a concerned look. "Do not worry, Madam. I'll investigate what's going on out there and arrange for you to vacate the premises. I shall return as soon as possible."

Honest to goodness, he talked like that, like some old-fashioned manual.

People rushed through, bumping into her.

She moved closer to the wall to keep out of the jostling flow. The last thing she needed was for her gown to be torn just before she went on stage. "I'll be in my dressing room," she called after Morin, but wasn't sure if the man heard her.

The hallway was clogged, people elbowing each other, some speaking languages she didn't understand. It seemed like the entire staff was back here for some reason, even the lighting assistant they'd passed earlier. She gave up fighting to get to her own dressing room and stepped inside the nearest storage room instead.

She closed the door and turned the rusty key in the lock. Her dressing room had looked brand-new, but this place didn't look renovated unless one counted the fresh coat of paint on the walls. She supposed all budgets had their limits. Money had probably been saved on out-of-the-way storage areas. She listened. If Morin called her name out there, she would be able to hear it.

Five minutes passed. She unlocked the door with some effort—the key was sticking—and, looking out, could see her dressing room. Morin wasn't there.

She pulled back in. Everything was going to be fine.

There had been some unrest in the country the year before, but peace had been restored. Since most of the royal family were to attend tonight's performance, security in and around the opera house was top-notch. Craig, her agent, and she had already discussed security concerns.

According to the tour she'd been given on arrival, the building had withstood three hundred years of turbulent history, including two world wars. She closed her eyes and tried to calm her breathing. She would be safe in here.

Small bottles of mineral water stood in a crate by the door. Looking at them made her realize how dry her mouth had gone from all the excitement. She grabbed a bottle and twisted the cap off, but didn't get a chance to drink before another explosion shook the building, this one closer than the first. Jars of stage makeup rattled on the desk.

She put her drink down, then stepped to the door and pushed the purple Bombay chest—must have been a prop at one point—in front of it, barricading herself inside. The din out in the hallway was disconcerting. Maybe the rebels were trying to fight their way in through the back entrance.

Craig was in the audience. She wished she could talk to her agent, but her cell phone was in her own dressing room. She wished Benedek hadn't left her. He would know what was going on, at the very least. His people would keep him informed.

She stayed near the door, listening. She was fine. Everything was fine. In a minute or two, Morin would be back.

"HOW SERIOUS IS THE situation?" Benedek asked again as he scanned the wall of monitors.

The director of security for the opera house was of the opinion that the peaceful protest at Liberation Square had been a ruse by the Freedom Council. The enemies of the monarchy had gathered as many of their people as possible in the vicinity of the opera house to sabotage the opening, perhaps even capture the royal family who were supposed to be in attendance.

Except that the Queen had felt unwell earlier in the evening, and Benedek's brothers lingered by her side, running late. She'd taken to her bed over a year ago, her condition fluctuating since. So when the crowd attacked, the princes were still safely at the palace. Benedek, who'd been here since early morning, making sure opening night would be a resounding success, was the only member of the royal family currently in the building.

"How many rebels are we talking about this time?" he asked, tacking another question onto the first before the director had a chance to answer.

"About two thousand is the best we can

estimate from the upper windows, Your Highness."

He nodded. At least Rayne got out in time and was inside the palace by now, under heavy guard. He barely had a half dozen royal guards here. The rest were supposed to arrive later, with his brothers. "Who's their leader?"

"A very angry young man, Your Highness. Goes by the name of Mario and fancies himself a freedom fighter. The palace just sent over a security report on him. Supposedly, he's not associated with the Freedom Council."

Maybe he hadn't been before, but Benedek had a feeling the Council had gotten to him and were using him now.

The three nameless men who ran the council were ruthless in their quest to dethrone the monarchy and break up the country, along ethnic lines, into small republics they would have full control over.

"Should I initialize lockdown?" The director waited for his answer.

The opera house had a massive security system in place. A computer program handled the entrances, all of which could be sealed at the push of a button. But if they locked down, it would be viewed as a step toward conflict, the crowd outside would be provoked and might lay siege to the building. He didn't want to risk the damage, not while they still had other options. "I'll try negotiating first."

The director paled. "I beg you to think of your safety, Your Highness. I shall go out there immediately."

"You stay here and keep people from panicking."

"Your Highness—" The man tried to stand in his way and stop him while remaining respectful and deferential, not an easy task.

The royal guards stepped closer as well. His new bodyguard didn't seem amused either.

"This is my opera house." Benedek gave them a level look. "Anyone wants to lay a finger on it, they answer to me."

Two bombs had already exploded outside.

The rebels, whatever they wanted, needed to know that he wasn't as easily intimidated as that. He hadn't started fighting yet. Before the evening turned into night, he would have the rebels gone and Rayne back on stage. Or else.

"THERE ARE THREE BOMBS in the building," the voice said on the other end of the line, playing his trump card over and over again, sounding triumphant and frustrated at the same time.

The call had come in on a red cell phone someone had left in the security office. Nobody there now knew who it belonged to or how it got there.

The dozen men inside the opera's security office watched Benedek intently, hoping for a resolution at last. He silently shook his head. That first bomb outside had exploded an hour ago and they hadn't yet gotten anywhere.

"Almost a thousand innocent people are in this building. Your quarrel is with the monarchy. This has nothing to do with tonight's audience. I'm the only member of the royal family here. You let these people go and I will willingly give myself into your hands," he repeated his best offer, and the men around him protested again.

Negotiations were at a deadlock. He'd been trying to talk reason into the man on the other end of the line on and off for the past hour, to no avail.

The enemy was frustrated because they'd

expected six princes and got only one instead.

"You say your revolution is for the people," Benedek reminded the man. "Then don't hurt the people, Mario. You can't think that the publicity to your cause would be anything but negative. If you want to gain public support, murdering a thousand innocent civilians is not the way to go about it. This isn't a glorious battle for freedom, you and I both know it. It's mass murder. Somebody is using you as a means to an end."

Dead silence on the other end.

"I'll let them walk out unharmed," the man said after a full minute, probably as frustrated with the stalled negotiations as Benedek. "But you will not leave the building. Not you, not that American singer."

And for the first time, Benedek relaxed. "She has nothing to do with this," he offered a token protest to make sure the man didn't become suspicious. Thank God, Rayne had left before the building had been surrounded.

Two thousand rebels circled the opera house; five hundred police as well as royal guards, investigators, antiterrorist unit agents and other security circled the rebels. Helicopters hovered in the air above—he could see and hear them through the window. He imagined the scene must look like a giant bull's eye from the air. With his opera house smack in the middle.

His muscles were tight with outrage.

Security forces couldn't move without risking that the rebels might set off the bombs. They were at an impasse.

Which would remain the same even after the people were let go. Security forces wouldn't risk the lives of their prince and a high-profile American by rushing the rebels. The rebels knew this.

"In exactly five minutes, a gap will open in our ranks directly across from the main entrance. Anyone who wants to leave the building, can walk through. They'll have five minutes to leave before the ranks close. Anyone outside after that, between us and the building, will be shot at," the voice on the phone said.

"There are a thousand people in here—" Benedek argued, wanting to negotiate for more time, but the line had already gone dead.

He glanced at his watch as he ran for the

door. "In five minutes, they'll let everyone leave," he said, explaining the rest as he went.

Security followed behind to help.

He rushed downstairs and straight to the stage, flying up the steps Rayne had stumbled on not long ago, falling into his arms. Thank God, whatever was about to happen here, no harm would come to her.

The sound was on, everything was ready for her performance. The audience was in their seats where they'd been asked to remain for their own safety. Benedek addressed them, explaining everything in two minutes flat. The next three were spent lining everyone up in front of the door in a tight line, ready to go.

His phone rang.

"What can I do to help?" his brother, Miklos the Army major, asked.

"Do *not* come here. They're letting people go. I'll call you back later." Benedek opened the front door, making sure that if there was foul play involved, his body would shield those behind him.

His security guard pushed him out of the way the next second, putting himself in front of Benedek. "This is what they want, Your Highness. Don't make yourself a target."

They watched as the rebel forces parted, leaving a five-foot gap to freedom.

"Run!" was the last word of advice Benedek gave to the men and women before stepping away from the door completely.

And they did, helping each other, careful not to cause a stampede, many speaking words of encouragement to their prince as they left. He'd never been as proud of his people as he was at that moment.

"Go!" he said again when he looked back inside the lobby and spotted the royal guards and a couple of other men who hadn't come up to the door.

He glanced at his watch. "Thirty seconds."

The rest of the staff and audience were already crossing to freedom, clearing the ring of rebels. A lady of his mother's age brought up the rear, running with her granddaughter in her arms. The little girl slowed her down too much, as did her gown. Benedek watched them, while yelling at the men who'd stayed behind. "You must leave! There's no time."

Two royal guards separated from the group and dashed out the door. One grabbed the young girl and ran; the other tossed the stately lady in her full-skirted brocade gown right over his shoulder and dashed forward with her.

They made it before the rebels closed ranks.

Benedek stepped away from the door and let it close, foreboding filling him as he took in the nearly empty space, the remains of his grand opening night. In hindsight, his hope that the delay wouldn't last more than an hour was probably too optimistic. He glared at the men.

"You should not have stayed." He drew a deep breath. "But I thank you for your loyalty," he told them.

"Should probably go back upstairs, Your Highness," one of the older royal guards recommended, and they followed him, seeing no purpose in lingering just inside the entrance.

When they made it back inside the security office, two of the guards immediately went to monitor the cameras set up inside and outside the building. Eight royal guards had remained, plus his personal security guard, plus the director, plus three civilians.

"Peter Havek, retired police officer," one of the civilians introduced himself.

"Tamas Havek, from Havek Construction.

Brothers, I have some demolition experience. We could go and look for those bombs. With your permission, Your Highness."

The director handed them each a headset, then they were on their way even as Benedek thanked them. The royal guards followed, except for the two who manned the monitors, looking for the bomb with the help of the security cameras. Over a hundred cameras had been strategically placed throughout the building.

"Craig Miller." The third civilian spoke with an American accent. "Rayne's agent. Where is she?" The man's lips were tight with worry, making Benedek wonder just what his relationship was with Rayne. He looked distinguished with just a touch of gray at the temples, wore an expensive tux and an expensive watch, standing apart from the others. "She doesn't answer her cell."

"My secretary escorted Miss Williams to the palace an hour ago." As soon as he had a second, Benedek was going to call and check on them. Maybe even now. He reached for his cell phone, then let it drop back into his pocket and turned when the computer behind him sounded a series of beeps.

The two royal guards at the main console were desperately pushing buttons.

"Security lockdown just self-initiated," one reported, casting about a wide-eyed look, disbelief in his voice.

"Impossible. It can't self-initiate." The director rushed over.

"Someone hacked into the system."

"I'll recall the damn lockdown." The director's voice rose, along with the color in his cheeks. "I apologize, Your Highness." He moved to a free console immediately. Seconds passed. "Whoever initialized it already changed the password." His tone was filled with outrage.

Benedek left Rayne's agent and stepped up to the director. "What does this mean, exactly?"

"We're locked in," the director told him. "Nobody goes out, nobody comes in."

"What do they want now? With them out there, we couldn't leave anyway—"

The red cell phone rang, cutting him off.

The man on the other end of the line said, "Bring Rayne Williams to the front door in twenty minutes. The door will open for one minute exactly and you will hand her over.

If she's not there when we open the door, we blow up the building. We've planted three bombs in the building."

Chapter Two

"This makes no sense," Craig said after Benedek had hung up the phone and explained everything to the men around him. "If they were going to let Rayne go, why didn't they let her go with the others?"

"They aren't planning on letting her go." Benedek's jaw clenched. "She's to be their high-profile hostage. This way they, or at least their leaders, can get away after they blow up the opera."

"With us in it?" Craig looked from one man to the other, wide-eyed.

The director of security nodded. "Your Highness must get out at any cost."

"But we don't have Rayne." Craig wiped his sweating hands on the side of his designer tux.

"We'll tell them that Miss Williams is

unwell," the director said, a speculative look coming into his eyes. "Play for time."

"Why?" Craig looked between the two men. "If we tell them that she's not here, maybe they won't blow up the building. Without a hostage, the second they make a move, security forces will massacre them. The rebels won't risk that. They won't do anything if they don't have her."

"Their main goal is to end the monarchy. They have me trapped. Whatever happens, they're not going to let me leave here." Benedek lay down the somber facts. "You shouldn't have stayed."

A moment of silence passed as each man considered what might happen next.

"We need time to find a way to get Prince Benedek out of the building," Benedek's security guard said. "If we tell them that Miss Williams isn't here, they might turn this into a suicide mission and blow up the building right now."

"I'm not going anywhere, unless we all go," Benedek stated flatly. "If we tell the rebels that Miss Williams is unwell, but will go out shortly, we might gain enough time to find the bombs and disarm them. It's in their best interest to wait for her. They'll want to wait."

"Why is that?" Craig asked.

"They think my brothers will rush to my rescue and then they can get all the princes." The absolutely maddening thing was that he knew his brothers *would* come. No amount of common sense, palace security, probably not even a royal order from the Queen would hold them back.

He had to solve this problem before that. He needed enough time to find and disarm the bombs with the help of their resident demolition expert, but not so much time that his brothers could come up with a plan and show up here. The difficulty was in the balance.

"Except, we can't call the rebels back to negotiate." The call had come in as an unregistered number and could not be redialed.

He'd been hotheaded enough at the beginning, so outraged by the attack that he'd wanted to rush out to give a piece of his mind to the bastards. He'd now cooled enough to realize that risking his life was not the best course of action. For one, if anything happened to him, his brothers for sure would be over here in the next second, starting a civil war.

"Now what?" Craig asked.

"Now we spread out and comb the building for those bombs." The director handed a headset to Benedek and one to Craig. Everyone else already had them.

With his bodyguard on his heels, Benedek took off toward the lower levels. Having worked on every detail of the renovations, he knew the building like he knew the names of all Valtrian kings back to the ninth century, the beginnings of the monarchy. First he went to the area that housed the furnaces and air conditioning. He checked under, behind, and on top of every piece of equipment.

Nothing, nothing, nothing.

His bodyguard helped, too, making the process faster. They went to the prop room next. Then costumes, tension growing in his shoulders as he moved from one area to the next. He walked through the giant backup pantry that would be used by the five-star restaurant that would soon open inside the opera house.

He checked his watch before moving on. They had less than five minutes left.

"Couldn't find anything," someone checked in over the headset.

"No bomb here either," another voice said.

Benedek's cell phone rang.

"Your Highness. I got caught up in a tussle behind the opera house and lost my phone," Morin, his secretary said. "I apologize for not being in touch sooner. I just got into the palace. Is there anything anyone can do from here?"

"Until further notice, your only job is to take care of Miss Williams."

"Your Highness?"

Something in his tone sounded the alarm for Benedek. "She's safe with you. Correct?"

"She didn't come with me, Your Highness. She wasn't let go with the other hostages? I just heard—forgive me, I just got in."

Benedek's blood ran cold at the thought of any harm coming to her. "She's probably with the chief of palace security."

"I just talked with him. He hasn't seen her."

His muscles tightened, his complete focus on the man on the other end. "Where did you see her last?"

"Just inside the back entrance."

Benedek ended the call and spoke into his headset. "Rayne Williams is in the building.

Start looking for her, keep looking for the bomb. I repeat, Rayne is in the building. Find her."

NOBODY HAD COME for her.

Nearly two hours had passed since Morin had left. She'd listened at the door, waiting for him to call her name in the hallway, but he hadn't. Nobody had. All noise had stopped, in fact, over an hour ago, as if all staff had cleared out.

She had tried to leave several times, but the ancient key had gotten stuck in the lock then broke right off when she'd tried to force it. She had shouted for help to the point of risking damage to her vocal cords, but nobody had answered.

And then, at last, she heard her name called.

"Rayne!"

She'd never been as glad to hear another sound in her life. She thought she recognized the voice. "Prince Benedek?"

The door handle rattled.

"It's stuck."

"Stand back," he said.

The door burst open with a bang in the next second.

"Are you all right?" He stood in the threshold like some theatrical hero, in his impeccable tux and with blazing eyes. She noticed again how tall he was, the breadth of his shoulders, the incredible depth of his gaze. His was the kind of presence critics called "mesmerizing" in a performance.

He was years younger than her, for heaven's sake.

She gathered herself and stomped out even the smallest spark of attraction. "Fine. Thank you." She smoothed her hair into place and lifted her chin. She hated anyone seeing her shaken.

His bodyguard stood outside in the hallway, inclined his head. "Madam."

Benedek took her hand without preamble and pulled her after him. Again, his touch was electrifying, his hand enfolding hers, warm and secure. She'd taken her gloves off earlier, and now found the skin-to-skin touch disconcerting.

"Where's everyone else?" The utter silence of the building had been making her increasingly nervous.

"The rebels let the audience leave. Only

fifteen of us stayed here. Including you. The building is locked down."

"So they can't get in?" Oh, good.

"So we can't get out."

Her lungs constricted. "We're trapped?"

The tight expression on his face was enough of an answer.

"Where are we going?" she asked, but he began talking into his headset, something she hadn't noticed earlier.

"I've got Rayne. We're on our way to the restaurant. Found any bombs yet?" He paused to listen. "Seek cover."

She went weak in the knees. "What bomb? Did they find it? What do you mean?"

"The rebels might have explosives in the building." He glanced at his watch and was now out and out running.

"Why are we going to the restaurant?" She ran up the stairs by his side.

He let her hand go so she could hold up the folds of her voluminous skirt with both hands and not trip. She no longer cared about wrinkling her gown before the performance. There would be no performance tonight. They would be lucky if they still had an opera house when this was all over. Or if they were still alive. She reached the top and dashed through the gilded swinging doors.

Benedek ran straight for the back. "Industrial meat cooler," he said, as if that explained anything.

Then they were through the kitchen and at the giant, stainless-steel doors. He pushed up the lever and opened the door. They just about fell inside, his bodyguard leaping in after them.

The first thing she registered was that the place was empty, the second that it wasn't freezing. Hadn't been turned on yet. Thank God, since her dress was rather open on top. Then the door slammed shut, and they were enveloped in darkness.

An explosion shook the building, ten times stronger than the previous two. Whatever blew up now had been a lot nearer.

She was about rattled off her feet, careful to put out a steadying hand toward the wall and not toward the prince. But his hand shot out in the darkness, went around her waist and secured her. He was so close that she could feel his heat, the strong, solid presence of his body. *Bombs,* he'd said earlier. There could be more. Even closer than the last one.

Oh, to hell with self-composure for once. She grabbed on to his arm in a death grip.

She disliked wealthy men of privilege on principle. She was even more wary of Benedek, who'd watched her with a singular intensity during her performances, and at times made it difficult for her to completely immerse herself in whatever role she was playing. No other man had ever been able to do that to her, and she resented his ability to mess with her head.

But right now he was the closest thing to hang on to, and hang on she did.

"Easy," Benedek said next to her ear, his warm breath fanning her neck, tickling its way down her skin.

Half of her was preparing for death. Her other half was…tingling.

He had a soapy scent, very expensive soap, masculine but non-obtrusive, with a trace of spice that made her want to lean closer to catch more. Instead, she peeled her fingers off his arm as her initial panic ebbed and took a deep, steadying breath from the opposite direction. She couldn't be losing her composure just because they'd touched. They weren't even alone, for heaven's sake.

When, after long minutes, no further explosions came, he moved away from her. The light came on the next second. He was standing by the door. He'd probably flipped the switch.

He exchanged a glance with his bodyguard, emotions swirling in his dark eyes. Anger, out-and-out fury, was dominant. Then something else came into his gaze when he looked at her. "Are you all right?"

She nodded, not trusting herself to speak. A bomb just went off in the building. This wasn't normally part of the whole *opera singer experience.* Lockdown or not, they needed to get the hell out of here. There had to be a way.

His bodyguard was already opening the door and checking outside.

"What are we waiting for?" she asked when Benedek hesitated for a moment.

"There are two more bombs," he said.

"I APOLOGIZE. If I'd known that something like this would happen, if I thought that the country wasn't a hundred percent safe, I would have never allowed you to come here," Benedek told her.

"Yes. Well." She seemed shaken, but was

covering it up admirably, holding her head high and her spine straight, as regal as any queen. "I can hardly blame you. I'm sure you didn't plan on getting blown up. What do they want?"

The kitchen was in shambles, chairs turned over, pots and pans scattered on the floor.

He shook his head. "We should find the others."

"What do they want?" She wasn't easily distracted.

"They want the monarchy gone," he said, as his headset crackled to life.

The director was asking, "Is everyone all right?"

"Fine here. I've got Rayne," he said.

One by one, everyone checked in, except the ex-cop. Benedek tried to remember his name. "Where's Peter?"

"He was heading to the gift shop to look for the bomb last I talked to him," the guy's brother said.

Foreboding filled him. "Where was the explosion?"

"East corner." The director's voice was glum.

Benedek moved forward. The east corner

of the building was where the gift shop was located. "Going there now."

His bodyguard stepped in the way immediately. "Your Highness—"

Benedek held up a hand. Someone was talking over the headset again.

"I'm almost there," the lost guy's brother, the construction expert, was saying. *Tamas.* Benedek remembered his name.

A few moments passed. "I'm there," the words crackled through Benedek's headset. Then came the scraping noise of something being pushed out of the way. Then a grunt. Then complete, utter silence. The man's voice sounded broken when he spoke next. "He didn't make it. No need to come here."

Benedek's jaw clenched. He relaxed it with some effort.

Originally, fifteen people had remained in the building after everyone else had left. With the ex-cop gone, they were down to fourteen.

"We lost a man." He passed on the news and reached for Rayne's hand, held it for a brief second before she pulled it back.

No more information was coming through his headset, the line was quiet. He wanted to ask of the damage to the building, but how could he do that? To Tamas, the damage was absolute. He had lost a brother. Benedek gave thanks to God that his brothers had been late to the performance, that they would be spared whatever was going to happen.

As long as they were smart enough to stay away. Unfortunately, knowing his brothers as he did, he highly doubted that.

"Ceiling caved in here," Tamas reported after a while, his construction-trained mind probably surveying even without conscious effort on his part. "Some walls collapsed, but all the load-bearing walls are still standing. No major damage to the structure. No breach in the outside wall to get us out of the place." He paused. "I'm going to stay here for a few more minutes."

To say goodbye. "Take all the time you need," Benedek said.

The siege of the opera house had its first victim. He wasn't optimistic enough to believe that the man had also been the last.

A MAN HAD DIED.

It brought everything into sharp focus, making their situation even more frighteningly real. Rayne followed Benedek back to the security office where he was supposed to meet the others.

"How did you know they were going to detonate the bomb?" The way he'd been running for cover, it was as if he'd known exactly what was going to happen.

"They gave us an ultimatum."

"Which was what?"

They were heading up the stairs. The prince remained silent.

"What ultimatum?"

He said nothing.

A man waited for them at the office door. Benedek introduced him as the director of security. Rayne wasn't impressed.

"What do the protesters want?" she asked without preamble, in a voice that told the guy that she expected a clear and honest answer.

"Right now, they want you, Madam." The man cast a nervous glance at the prince.

The words left her speechless.

"You're not going anywhere," the prince reassured her immediately.

Which was exactly what she'd been thinking, but she would have liked to be the one to decide that. "What on earth would they want with me?" She had no connection to this country, none whatsoever.

The prince explained with some reluctance.

A hostage. So they could get away after they killed him. And he was so insanely calm. Youth. It had to be that. He just didn't comprehend how much danger he was in. Then again, he didn't seem like a man who missed much. He had keen, sharp eyes that shone with intelligence. And desire if he looked at her for more than a second. She so did not want to have to deal with that.

And she wouldn't have to if the rebels took her as a hostage so they could kill him.

She had to sit down. The folds of her gown draped over the chair, nearly making it disappear under the billowing material. Her brain chugged along at a snail's pace.

He was to be killed.

"Hell of a country," she said to herself.

"The best in the world." Benedek's eyes flashed. "Which doesn't mean that we don't have a few malcontents."

"Odd, but I don't recall civil unrest and murderous tendencies being mentioned in my pre-trip briefing. Must have missed a page," she snapped, angry at the whole situation and that he would defend the very people who tried to kill him.

"You'll be safe," he promised, his tone instantly milder.

Men were coming into the room—the royal guard. A cell phone rang in Benedek's pocket. Small and red, she saw when he took it out, handling it as if it were a poisonous snake. Tension immediately doubled as everyone held their breath.

The prince answered the call and listened. "She needs a little more time. She's almost ready." He pulled the phone away from his ear. "We got ten more minutes."

"Freezer?" she asked.

"Not enough room for everyone," he said.

The director touched his headset and spoke into it. "Tamas? Are you there?" He waited a few seconds as more royal guards came in.

Thirteen people were in the room now. Tamas was the only one missing.

"Tamas? Do you need help?" the director asked, then said after a short pause. "There's no response."

"The security cameras are out in that corner of the building since the explosion," a guy sitting by the row of monitors said.

They all spoke English, albeit with various accents, probably as a courtesy to her.

"I'll go over there and see if he needs anything." Another man got up to leave.

"We'll all go." Prince Benedek looked around at the people in the room. His body-guard was scowling, but nobody questioned Benedek's authority. She couldn't imagine they would, and not because he was a prince. The man had a powerful presence and the aura of a leader. "It might be the safest place yet," he went on. "The bomb in that section already exploded. Who knows where the others are?"

It made terrifying sense.

One of the older guards, Vilmos she thought his name was, protested some more that the prince should stay in the security office with some guards, but Benedek overrode him.

They trooped down the stairs then, through deserted hallways. The prince kept close to her. She found that she didn't mind.

In a minute or two, they could see the first signs of damage, cracked walls and floor tile, then, as they turned the corner, the gift shop came into view. The ceiling had collapsed, wires hung from the wall, everything was covered in dust and rubble. It was the first visual they got of what that bomb had done, and it painted a scary future.

A body lay propped against one wall.

"Peter." The director hurried over.

"Tamas." The prince was ducking behind a chunk of busted wall.

She followed him and saw a man down just as the prince bent to check for a pulse. His face held so much cold anger that she drew back.

"What happened to him?"

He moved away, and she could see the bloodstain on the man's shirt. Small cut, big stain.

"Knife wound," someone spoke from behind her, and her head reeled.

The prince looked over the small group, even as his bodyguard moved closer to him. "Nobody goes anywhere on their own. They have a man in the building somewhere."

He meant the rebels had a killer in the building. She glanced around, surprised at how well everyone else was taking the news. Meanwhile, her heart was racing so fast she could barely catch her breath.

Dark thoughts chased each other inside her head. The rebels didn't trust their bombs one hundred percent. They had a backup plan, insurance, someone on the inside who could take out their small group, one by one if necessary, until he got to the prince.

"We'll stay together," Benedek was saying, taking control again. "We'll be fine."

But something told her they wouldn't be.

They were trapped in a building rigged with some serious explosives.

And they were being hunted.

Chapter Three

"Have you looked out the window lately?" Miklos asked over the phone.

"Looking right now," Benedek said. The rebel forces seemed to have dwindled. "What's going on out there?"

They were back in the security office. At least from here they could keep track of the building with the help of the security cameras. No movement anywhere. Where in hell was the bastard who'd killed Peter and Tamas?

"The protest was staged by the Freedom Council. It's confirmed."

Benedek swore. He'd suspected as much.

"Some paid agitator stirred up the crowd," Miklos continued. "Half of them didn't know the real reason why they were marching on the opera house. They thought they were protesting new tax burdens. Now that the true reason is out, many are deserting the protest."

"Even if every one of them leaves, the bombs remain. And we'll still be locked in here."

"We're working on that." Miklos's voice sounded tight. "I have the bomb squad on standby. The second you find anything, you call."

"We have other problems. Two men are dead in here." Benedek told him who they were. "I think there's an enemy inside."

A moment of silence on the other end, then, "Could be that was their backup plan."

"Or could be that was plan A. Surround the building, announce the bomb scare, and in the resulting chaos, an assassin could have killed the royal princes. Maybe using the bombs was the backup, in case the assassin didn't succeed."

"Except that we were late. You're the only prince there."

"And I want to keep it that way. I'm trusting you to keep our brothers at the palace."

"Believe me, I've had my hands full with that. I had to wrestle Lazlo to the ground, not that I mind showing him who's boss now and then."

Benedek relaxed for a second, thinking about his twin. Then realized that if Miklos was keeping the others at the palace, that meant he was planning on coming over all alone, because there was no way Miklos could stay out of this. "Before you do anything crazy, think of your wife and your son." It was the only leverage Benedek had.

"Don't you worry about me, little brother."

It wasn't exactly the reassurance he needed to hear.

They didn't talk long before hanging up. Benedek was putting the phone away just as the red cell rang.

"Time is up. I'm about to deactivate the lock on the front door. I better see Rayne Williams coming through there."

The line went dead before Benedek could have demanded that the bastard call off his inside man. Not that he thought the guy would suddenly turn reasonable. But he would have liked to at least try and talk some sense into him given the chance.

"What is it?" the director asked.

"Same demand as before."

"You should let them have me." Rayne stood from her chair with a rustling of fabric, determination on her face. She looked like a heroine from some century-old legend. "It'd be a distraction. Maybe the security forces could grab the rebel leaders."

Some of the guards kept staring at her when they thought she wasn't looking. Benedek couldn't blame them. She did look spectacular, as regal as any queen and sexy as hell in that low-cut bodice. Craig stood close to her, patting her hand now and then.

The gesture irritated Benedek—and so did the warm looks she shot back. "I can't guarantee your safety, so no." That she would even think that he would let her walk into danger...

She didn't look happy with him, but after a moment said, "Even if we don't all fit into that meat locker, you at least should go in there. You're the prince."

"She's right, Your Highness," his bodyguard immediately voiced his support.

He glanced at his watch. "Safe's closer."

"What safe?" Rayne was blinking at him.

"I haven't received the new code this morning, Your Highness." The director's lips flattened.

"I have it." Benedek was already heading

toward the back. He opened a door that revealed a steel panel, and keyed in a code, then waited impatiently for the steel panel to open.

"WHY DOES AN OPERA HOUSE have a bank safe?" Rayne went in first as all the men motioned her forward, and she didn't feel like arguing. The inside looked like flea market storage, which, under other circumstances, she would have appreciated. She had a weakness for flea markets and everything old.

"It's a three-hundred-year-old opera house," the director explained. "We have a lot of valuable antiques, furniture, paintings, Persian rugs that are hundreds of years old and worth hundreds of thousands. We use the safe when there's work being done in the building. Also, the artwork in the hallways and rotunda are rotated continuously as pieces are restored. Some are stored here."

The place was fairly full. With thirteen people on top of all those valuables, it was pretty crowded. Somehow Prince Benedek came to be standing behind her. As more people came in, she had no choice but to back up until her back was pressed against him. He was nearly a head taller than she, so her bare shoulders rested against his hard chest.

Normally, someone standing that close would have bothered her but under the circumstances, she felt comforted by his nearness. Comforted and something else, not that she was prepared to admit that.

Especially when she realized that she could feel his breath on her neck, that all he would have to do was dip his head to press his lips to her skin. What a stupid, stupid thing to think.

He would never do that. Why would he? So he'd sent her some flowers over the years, but he was hardly desperate. He probably had a dozen mistresses—the privilege of wealthy men. She pushed her ex-husband from her mind. Her marriage was over. She'd wasted enough years on Philip. She didn't want to think of him ever again.

Minutes ticked by in tense silence.

The small space grew warm from their body heat. The day had been unseasonably warm for spring. She held still, not wanting to move against Benedek, but she was aware of their bodies touching, aware of every breath he took. A drop of sweat rolled down her neck. She hoped he wouldn't notice that.

Heat grew inside her as well. Insane. They were fully clothed and in the middle of a crowd. She wasn't the type to have her knees go weak at the sight of a man or from a touch. She wasn't what they called sensuous. She'd accepted that over the years. It wasn't important.

But if she did have some hidden side, couldn't it have come out for any other man but him? She was done with rich and powerful men, and he was richer and more powerful than any that she'd met.

The building shook. The prince's strong arms came to hold her around her waist like before. Without conscious thought, she put her hands over his, like before, feeling rattled for more than one reason.

Her body didn't miss a thing, no matter how loudly her mind protested.

"Basement," the director said, guessing the location of the bomb.

"I didn't get around to checking every room down there," Benedek said.

He'd been down there with the bomb? Her

hand squeezed his without her meaning to do it.

"The good news is, the building is still standing." He didn't move away. "One more bomb and they have nothing to threaten us with."

The director, in front, was pushing the safe door open. Since there was barely air to breathe in there, they came out, but stayed close by.

The red cell rang. Benedek put it on speaker.

"I'm tired of firing warning shots. The next one is going to be a big one. Make no mistake, it *will* bring down the building. You have forty-five minutes to think about it." Once again, the line went dead as soon as the last word was spoken.

She was the one the rebels wanted. At least for now. She drew a deep breath and steeled her spine, turned to face Benedek.

"If I go out, maybe it'll cause enough of a distraction so that you and the others can escape through a window in the back. I know you don't like this plan, but we don't have much choice."

"The lower level windows have wrought-iron bars," he said, not looking the least amused by her repeated suggestion.

Of course. She remembered now that she'd admired the exquisite workmanship. "Maybe you could rappel down from a second story window on something."

"No." Benedek's response was as inflexible as those iron bars.

"Your Highness, you must consider." His bodyguard took her side.

In fact, judging from the men's faces, it looked like everyone except Craig supported her. He came over to put a hand on her arm. "No, Rayne. You can't give yourself to the rebels. You don't know that they wouldn't harm you."

Craig was always on her side. He was the only man in the world whom she unconditionally trusted, even if he did push her maybe a little too much at times to make nice with the opera's most generous patrons. He'd set up this trip, in fact. She had trusted him as a partner in business, but not until now did she realize the depth of his loyalty and how much he cared for her. She put her hand on his and squeezed, knowing that all he wanted was to keep her safe.

Something flickered in Benedek's hard gaze, but it was gone before she could identify it.

"And when the rebels figure out that they've been tricked and kill you without a second thought?" His voice was clipped.

"I—" All she could think of was that she was known around the world, a celebrity in her field. Would these men really do that?

"I'm not going to consider that option." He held her gaze until her skin heated.

SHE LOOKED FIERCE AND lost at the same time. Benedek had no idea how she managed it, but the look was breathtaking and disarming. Oh, yeah, and it made him want her. He really was becoming rather pitiful about that.

She drew a deep breath that nearly sent her breasts spilling over the rim of that ridiculous gown. He was mesmerized. Had a feeling there wasn't a man in the room who hadn't noticed.

"Let's find that bomb then," she said. "We have no time to waste."

He nodded and looked around. "Rayne and Craig stay here." He motioned toward the safe. "The rest will pair up in twos." He looked toward others, eight guards and the director, plus his bodyguard.

"Your Highness will stay as well?" the director asked.

"I know this building better than anyone here."

"Your Highness should take two men. Allow me—"

He cut off the protest with a motion of his hand. "Then we'd only have six teams instead of seven. My way we'll cover ground faster."

"We'll go with you and there'll still be seven. If the next explosion is a large one, the safe's not going to be much help. For you to go alone would definitely not be the smartest thing." Rayne came to stand in front of him again.

She had never hesitated to face him or to say whatever she thought made sense instead of whatever she thought he wanted to hear. He liked her candor.

Which didn't mean that he was going to allow her to tag along.

But beyond the straight set of her shoulders, beyond the brave face she'd put on from the beginning, he could at last see in her silver eyes that she was scared. And knew at once that the argument was over. He could never leave her behind if she felt safer going with him.

"Very well."

The director was already dividing his

people into teams and assigning areas to search. Craig was assigned to Vilmos, an older guard who'd had his eyes on Rayne way too much for Benedek's taste.

"We'll take the hall by the back door," Benedek said and took off that way with Rayne and his bodyguard. He dialed his brother Miklos as they moved forward, keeping their eyes open for the slightest suspicious thing as they went. "Forty-five minutes. The latest threat is a bomb big enough to bring down the building."

"Bomb squad is on standby with me right here. We're in the armored car at the edge of the park if you get a chance to look out the back. They'll walk you through how to disarm it. Just find it and call."

"I'm working on that. You get back to the palace. How is Mother?"

The momentary silence on the other end of the line told him that her condition was once again worsening.

"Dr. Arynak is with her."

They'd almost lost her last year. She hung on by sheer will to see her first grandchild being born. The joy of that little boy kept her alive these days.

The Queen didn't need the stress of knowing what was going on at the opera house. His brothers would do their best to shield her, but she would sense their upset and the tension in the air. She would sense it and worry.

They exchanged a few more words before disconnecting. He stepped over a large light fixture that had crashed to the floor in the middle of the hallway, probably from the force of one of the explosions. He immediately looked up to check the others in case walking under them was unsafe, but only this one seemed to have been loosened.

"Careful." He offered his hand to Rayne to help her step over the fixture and the broken glass. Shards crunched under their feet.

For a second her fingers tightened around his. Then the hem of her gown got caught on the fixture and as she yanked it, her feet slipped on the shards and she stumbled. He dipped with her and caught her against him, raised her back up, but not before she'd braced a hand to the floor, cutting herself.

He took in her slim palm with dismay, hating to see her hurt. "There should be a first aid kit in the security office. I need that," he ordered his bodyguard.

The man hesitated.

"Either you go, or I will and you stay here with Miss Williams."

"Your Highness, under the circumstances—"

"I can protect myself. Give me one of your guns. I'll be right here when you get back."

Looking decidedly unhappy, the man handed him a standard-issue Beretta then took off. Benedek tucked the weapon into his cummerbund, knowing the guy had a backup weapon so he wouldn't be walking the corridors unarmed either.

"It's not that bad," Rayne was saying.

Like hell it wasn't.

Benedek cursed himself as he examined her palm, the small pieces of glass embedded in her tender skin and the faint rivulets of blood. He wished she had kept her satin gloves on.

Her small hand gave a slight tremble in his, the only sign of the pain she must have felt. They were standing a short distance from the bathrooms. "Let's wash it off first." He drew her that way, pushed the door open and went right in with her.

She extracted her hand from his and ran cold water on it.

He checked the bathroom for any sign of a bomb while she did that, returning to her in short order. The stream dislodged most of the glass, leaving only the largest of the shards still embedded in her skin. She tried to remove it, biting her lower lip.

The sight of those white teeth sunk into moist, red flesh held him immobilized for a second.

"Wait." He cleared his throat. "Let me try." And he moved to take back her hand.

She hesitated. She barely knew him, had no reason to trust him. He felt a small sense of triumph when she put her hand in his anyway.

He wished he could distract her with something. Like a kiss. Her lips were ruby velvet, closer to his than they'd ever been. His breathing slowed as his gaze glided over those lips then lifted higher.

Her silver eyes widened as if she could read his mind.

The air thickened between them.

"It's not going to happen," she said, quite clearly.

She didn't need to spell out what she meant. The electric charge in the air between them threw about sparks, their connection a near palpable thing.

"Isn't it?" He dipped his head the short distance it took to brush his lips across hers.

He tugged the shard free in that very second.

She turned and pulled away, rinsing her palm again, then dabbing it dry with some paper towels. But as soon as she dabbed the blood, more beaded in her palm. She worked at that with efficient movements. "I have a rule against dating opera patrons." She wouldn't look at him.

He shouldn't want her this badly. Anything permanent between them was impossible. Short of that, a long, public affair would be scandalous. But he didn't seem to care. Realization dawned on him that he wanted Rayne any way he could get her.

A dangerous thought. He had to be careful there.

"My bodyguard should be here soon. Let me help." He took a few paper towels, put them together and folded them in quarters, pressed them against her palm then sandwiched her hand between his, applying pressure.

A long moment passed.

"Thank you." She looked at their hands, not at him.

"The bleeding should stop in a minute. We'll disinfect and bandage when the guard gets back."

She did look at him then. "Shouldn't he be here already?"

Yes, but he'd been trying to ignore that and the foreboding that spread over him. Like he was ignoring his body's demand to pull her into his arms. "Let's give him another minute." He kept the pressure on her hand.

The minute passed.

"Should we go back and look for him?" she asked as she pulled away and checked under the paper towels. The bleeding had stopped. She pressed the makeshift bandage back.

"We can't afford to go back. We have to cover our share of the building. He knows where we're headed. He can catch up with us."

They left the women's room, turned into the men's so he could check that for the bomb, then moved down the hallway. He opened the first dressing room.

"Any idea what the bomb would look like?" Rayne asked from behind him. She was pretending hard that they hadn't kissed.

"Large. Something powerful enough to bring down this building would have to be pretty damn large." He wanted to be with her anywhere but here.

They progressed through the rooms rapidly, searching through costume closets inside and any large prop boxes outside in the hallways. He double-checked Rayne's dressing room when they reached it.

"You can take a minute to change if you'd like," he told her when he was sure there was nothing dangerous in there.

She'd been dragging the full-skirted heavy brocade gown around without complaint, but he'd noticed how it slowed her down. It had to tire her out, too. Not that he wouldn't miss the low-cut bodice once she changed into something else. The picture of her full breasts in that thing was permanently imprinted on his brain.

It was a sight he was sure he'd see in his dreams again. He hoped.

He shifted through the props and found a silver silk scarf, the color an exact match to her eyes. "Here." He carefully wrapped it around her hand to keep the paper towels in place. "That should help."

He was about to step away from her when he realized that the bodice of her dress buttoned in the back, in the old style. Since she had no costume changes for this night, they could afford to go with historical accuracy instead of the Velcro and zippers that singing in a full opera would have required.

One of the dressing assistants must have helped her put the dress on. She couldn't get it off alone, not with her hand all bandaged.

"Let me assist with your dress."

IF SHE HAD A PENNY FOR every time she'd been offered that by a man with a hungry gleam in his eyes after a performance... Rayne blinked the thought away. She'd made plenty of money with her singing. She didn't need those pennies. Neither did she need another man in her life.

Still, she only hesitated a split second before turning her back to Benedek.

Changing would take only a minute. They would waste more time than that if her dress slowed them down, if it got caught on everything and tripped her wherever she went.

His hands were sure and skillful, moving rapidly down her back. She ignored the feel of his fingertips dragging against her skin as the material parted. When the bodice opened like a shell in the back, she held it to her front to keep it from dropping. She didn't wear a bra underneath, couldn't with this cut of the neckline, not without spoiling the whole authentic effect.

"Thank you."

She felt his hands move to her waist and untie the wide sash that held the top layer of the skirt, then the safety pins that held the series of petticoats under it. She sank to a large pine chest, the closest piece of furniture to her, to prevent the material from dropping around her ankles and leaving her in her underwear. Her skin tingled with awareness. He was inches from her and she was practically naked.

Her nipples were pointy, hard knobs. From the chill in the air, she told herself, although the temperature in her dressing room was nothing if not comfortable.

"I'd rather not leave you alone, not even to stand right outside the door." His voice sounded a little off. So little that no one but a singer trained to notice the tiniest nuance in any sound would have caught that.

"Of course," she said, annoyed that he would play that cheap trick. But she didn't have time for modesty. If they didn't get on with their search, find the bomb and disarm it in the next twenty-five minutes, they would all be dead.

She let the bodice drop first, keeping her back to him, and reached for the closest thing on the back of another chair, a T-shirt with the Valtrian Royal Palace on it that she'd received that morning as a gift from one of the staff. The material caught on her signature black pearl choker she never took off except for sleep. But all it needed was a tug before the material slipped free. The shirt was a size too small, fitting her like a second skin, the large image of the palace barely disguising the fact that she was too chicken to cross the room half-naked to retrieve her bra from the built-in closet.

The room felt hotter than a polar bear costume. The awareness between them was growing to an unbearable level. She half expected to feel his hands on her shoulders any second.

She stood with a nervous jump and let the skirts drop, grabbed a pair of fitted black pants someone had brought from the dry cleaners and hadn't put away yet. One of her suitcases had had an unfortunate accident with a makeup jar on the flight here. She slipped into the pants, then turned.

Prince Benedek stood with his back to her clear across the room, his wide shoulders silhouetted against the busy paisley pattern of the wallpaper.

He hadn't watched her dress.

She felt about as impressed as disappointed.

She slipped into a pair of silk loafers, the nearest footwear. "Ready." She headed for the door.

"Wait." His voice sounded husky as he cut in front of her and checked outside before they left. But then he let her go first, a gentleman.

"Where do you think your bodyguard is?" She'd half hoped to spot him somewhere in the hallway. She couldn't not think of Peter and Tamas, the men they'd already lost.

He shook his head, a somber look coming over his face. "We don't have time to look for him."

They searched through the dressing rooms together. And after a few minutes, she could actually breathe normally again.

"Where should we go next?" she asked when they reached the end.

"Downstairs."

"But that's where the second bomb was. Wouldn't the third be someplace else?" And Craig and that royal guard had already gone there.

"It's a large basement, there's room enough for two bombs. And if they'd been placed far enough from each other, with enough walls between them, one wouldn't necessarily set off the other."

Good point. She followed him down the stairs, feeling a lot more comfortable out of her dress, glad that soon they'd be with Craig and that other man. Being alone with Benedek was getting to be too much for her frayed nerves. It was one thing resisting him from afar, it was quite another fighting to keep from falling under his spell when he was within reach of her.

When they reached the steel door that led to the basement, he stopped for a second to turn back to her. "We'll find the bomb. We'll make it out of here." He tucked a stray lock of her hair behind her ears, his fingers gentle.

She wasn't used to her body responding so vehemently to a man.

A smile stretched his sexy, masculine lips as if he knew exactly what she was thinking, what she was feeling. "I've never seen anyone with as many walls built around her as you have," he observed. "Makes a man that much more curious."

She needed every one of her walls when she was around Benedek, but she shrugged as if she didn't know what he was talking about, then she went around him, ready to walk through that door. They needed to end this conversation before she did or said something that betrayed just how much of an effect he had on her.

He drew her back and pulled her behind him as if protecting her was some sort of an instinct with him. He turned the knob and called back to her over his shoulder, his voice low. "Word of warning."

"Yes?"

"I'm good with walls, Rayne."

Of course, he was. He was an architect. She had to remember to build a moat when she had a minute. And reinforce her walls. Definitely.

Her musings were interrupted when he pushed the steel door open and swore, putting a hand up to hold her back.

She pushed in behind him anyway.

Not far from the door, the outside wall of the basement had collapsed. Bricks lay in heaps. A gaping hole yawned where the wall had once stood. From what she could make out, it looked like there was a tunnel back there. But a still shape next to the piles of rubble soon dragged her attention from everything else.

"Craig!" She flew forward, ducking as Benedek tried to hold her back. She ran toward her agent, praying for him to open his eyes and look at her, even as she knew that he wouldn't.

Craig, the only friend she'd had in a long time, was dead. She couldn't not think that he was only here because of her in the first place. This was all her fault, just like the death of her mother and her brother had been. Not for the first time, she wished she were the one who'd died instead.

She cradled Craig's head and held him

tight. "I'm sorry. I'm so sorry," she whispered over and over again, knowing that nothing she could say or do would bring Craig back.

The killer was out there, and there was no way of telling who would be his next victim.

When a noise came from the tunnel, she spun that way, but couldn't see anything through her veil of tears.

Chapter Four

Benedek stood between her and the tunnel, ready to defend her. But the man who slowly took shape in the clouds of dust, stumbling forward among the rubble, was Vilmos, the royal guard who'd been Craig's search partner.

"Your Highness. Anything?" He coughed.

Nobody was coming up behind him. Benedek relaxed, but kept an eye on the tunnel, made sure it was in his line of vision at all times. It could still hold some unpleasant surprises.

With the next step forward, Vilmos spotted Craig. "What's wrong with him?" He rushed to him, tripped over a sizable chunk of cement and ended up on his knees next to Rayne.

"Craig?" He grabbed the man's shoulder. "I told him to come in with me. Not to separate." He shot Benedek a tight look, probably worried he'd be blamed. "I had to investigate the tunnel, Your Highness. It could be our way out or a way for the rebels to get in. I had to—"

"You did fine." Benedek set him at ease. "You did the right thing."

Rayne was holding her agent's head on her lap, tears rolling down her cheek. Her face was so tight he thought it might break. She didn't cry out, didn't sob. She held her emotions with an iron will, except for those few escaping tears.

He moved toward her to comfort her. She caught the move and shook her head slightly. Her walls were standing as strong as ever.

He hated to see her in pain.

Benedek tamped down his anger at whoever had killed her agent in cold blood, his gaze focusing on the large bloodstain on Craig's chest. "How long have you been in the tunnel?"

Vilmos looked dazed. "Less than five minutes. He was fine when I went in."

"Anything in there?"

"Old walls and rubble. It led someplace at some point, but the walls have mostly collapsed. I don't think there's an exit that way." His gaze returned to Craig. "I can't believe this happened. He didn't even call out. I would have heard him." He pushed to standing, running his fingers through his hair over and over again.

He was a trained guard, but a royal guard. Benedek doubted the man had had to face anything worse than a nosy tourist now and then since he'd received his palace appointment. Until recently, the kingdom had lived in peace. The only armed conflict, over a year ago, had happened in the mountains, at Maltmore Castle.

"It's not your fault," Benedek told him and stepped toward Rayne, extending a hand. "We better get back."

He tried to reach his bodyguard again over his headset, but the man didn't respond, so he shared his dark news with the others through their radio connection.

They were halfway up the stairs when a voice came over his headset. "Found the bomb. It's big enough to take off the two top floors, at least."

And the weight of those would collapse the rest of the building. "Where are you?"

"In the attic. Above the security office."

So the safe was out as a hiding place. Benedek glanced at his watch. Ten minutes left before the rebels' deadline. Not enough time for him to get to the attic, let alone to make contact with the bomb squad and disarm the bomb following phone directions.

He stopped and looked back toward the tunnel, then at Rayne's mascara-smudged eyes. Craig had been her agent. Of course, she cared for the man. It shouldn't bother him, Benedek thought. He shouldn't have such need to know whether they'd been only business associates, or something more.

She was not his. She could never be his, not for good. He needed to keep remembering that. But just because she wasn't his, it didn't mean that he wasn't going to save her. Or die trying.

"Everyone to the basement. Immediately," he told the men over his headset.

THERE WERE ONLY ELEVEN of them left. They had lost four men, one by one to an unseen killer. The thought had that eerie, horror-movie feel to it. The tunnel provided the perfect setting to take the grim story further.

Catacombs, Benedek had called the place. The very word was full of foreboding.

Rayne trudged forward in the semidarkness, the dank space lit only by the flashlights some of the royal guards carried.

The good news was Vilmos had been wrong and the tunnel hadn't collapsed completely. They had been able to dig through some rubble and enter the underground labyrinth behind it. At least the rebels hadn't blown up the opera house. Yet.

The bad news was that the small group moving deeper into the catacombs had no idea where they were or whether the narrow corridors they traveled would ever take them out of there. Also, the rebels *could* blow the building at any time, sealing them in forever. But possibly the worst part was that cell phones didn't work down here, so they were now completely cut off from the outside.

Nobody knew where they were.

Nobody could help them.

She'd heard of the catacombs of Rome when she'd sung there ages ago. She'd declined the tour that had been offered. "What is this place exactly?" she asked Benedek, who was walking in front of her.

Two royal guards went before him, two walked behind her, the director of opera security bringing up the rear.

"Palace Hill is riddled with catacombs. Some of them have been mapped, others haven't. This is a new section nobody knew about before."

He sounded suspiciously like maybe he was enjoying this just a little. Couldn't be. Every nerve ending she had was on edge. They'd practically been buried alive. Nobody could be excited about that.

"It's a brand-new discovery," he said.

And she definitely caught a note of excitement in his voice this time. She bit back a groan. He probably fancied himself some great underground explorer now. All she wanted was to get out of here.

His eyes danced as he looked back at her.

She caught herself before she shook her head. He was a boy at heart still. A young prince at thirty two.

Then his gaze changed, wrapped her up somehow, and made her think they were the only two people within miles, drew her in. Awareness was a like a caress on her bare skin. *A man,* she corrected. Whatever boyish pleasures he took in discovering these tunnels, Prince Benedek was all man, head-to-toe.

If only she were ten years younger…

She gave herself a mental shake. She also broke the eye contact between them, studiously examining the rough ground they trod. Within a few feet, they came to a Y in the tunnel.

"Which way?" one of the men asked.

"We could split up," Vilmos suggested. "Better chance of finding a way out that way." He still sounded anxious.

Rayne avoided his gaze, and he avoided hers. She tried not to be mad at him for leaving Craig all alone, but failed, even knowing she wasn't being completely reasonable.

Her eyes burned every time she thought of her agent. She blinked back the tears. She didn't cry. She wasn't the crying type. What was wrong with her?

"Except that we would have no way to keep in touch with each other." Benedek thought for a minute. "We'll stay together." He walked a short distance into each tunnel, came back.

"What are you doing?" Rayne asked.

"The left is sloping down, the right is sloping up. We'll take the right branch. It's more likely that it'll take us to the surface."

They moved ahead as fast as they could, watching where they stepped, the men grim and quiet. The tunnel soon narrowed and began to take turn after turn. At times, she had a feeling they were going in circles.

She wondered what the rebels must think now that they couldn't reach them on the phone. "How far are we from the opera house?"

"We walked at least two kilometers, but we could be right under it somewhere if the tunnel looped back around," Benedek told her. "Do you need to rest?"

"No."

He watched her for a second. "We'll rest," he called out to the men and stopped.

Men listened so well, she thought, and flashed him a forced smile.

"Let me see your hand." He was reaching for it before she could protest, turning her hand over in his larger palm and untying the scarf, examining the cuts. "It'll be fine."

She could have told him that. She could barely feel her injuries anymore. Under the circumstances, they were the least of her problems.

The two guards in the front walked back

to them, then the ones in the back started catching up. Dezso first, then Vilmos. They waited in vain for the director.

"I'll go and see what's holding him up," Vilmos offered.

"No," Benedek said immediately, his shoulders stiffening. "We can't afford to lose another."

Did they lose the director?

The somber look on Benedek's face confirmed that he was thinking the same thing—the killer had followed them into the catacombs.

For once, she didn't mind Benedek's nearness. She stayed where she was, reluctant to step away from him. The light dimmed. She glanced around. Dezso's flashlight was out. The batteries in the others wouldn't last forever either.

"We'll be fine." Benedek looked right at her as he said that. "This tunnel has to end somewhere."

She prayed it wasn't a dead end.

With a killer at their back.

"Maybe we shouldn't stop," she offered.

Benedek glanced at his watch. "Five minutes. Sit."

The men obeyed him without hesitation. After a moment, she did, too. He was right, they needed to catch their breath. Who knew how long they would have to wander around underground before finding a way out? And if they stayed put for a little while, maybe the director would catch up with them.

He didn't.

And soon it was time to go.

Two security guards in front of her and the prince, two in the back.

"Wait. The enemy is behind us. All security should be in the back," Dezso recommended.

For a moment, Benedek looked like he might protest. With each man that'd gone missing or was found dead, his expression became darker and darker. Even his pleasure over the secret tunnel discovery wore off within minutes. He looked ten years older now than when he'd first walked into her dressing room. But he still stood strong, decisive and ready to face whatever crossed their path.

In the end, he didn't argue with Dezso. All he said was, "Stay close together, don't leave anyone behind." Then he led his dwindling team forward into the unknown.

When they came into a narrower section with plenty of blind turns that would only allow one person at a time to pass, he took her hand. She didn't resist, although she couldn't remember the last time she had trusted herself to a man. Maybe never. The sensation now was not comfortable.

"You think the walls look good, Your Highness?" one of the men asked from behind. He had the oddest name that she couldn't, for the life of her, recall.

Benedek had been panning his flashlight along the walls and ceiling more than on the ground since they'd entered the tunnels. "These walls have been standing for three hundred years. It's statistically unlikely that they would collapse just at this very moment." He thought for a second. "Then again, we've had two explosions so far today that shook the ground around the opera. Still, I think we're far enough now."

So did she. While the tunnel took wild turns, they had been heading in one general direction for a while now.

"It wouldn't hurt to step carefully anyway," Benedek added.

The man asked something about the catacombs under the palace. They were talking mostly to keep in touch, to make sure that no one else from the end of the line disappeared. The prince had an easy rapport with the men. She hadn't pictured him being like that. She'd had royalty attend her performances before, had even been introduced to the Queen of Denmark. But she'd never spent this much time with anyone royal. He wasn't aloof or demanding. He was just like any other man.

Well, maybe not. He wasn't quite like any other man she had known. She had to admit, he was shattering her misconceptions about him one after the other. He did what he had to. He wasn't spoiled. He cared about his men.

"There's something up ahead." He slowed.

Her heart picked up speed.

But all he was referring to was an enlarged area they were approaching, a room their narrow tunnel came to before it continued on the other side. There were large, square holes carved in the walls all the way from the floor to the ceiling, with stone boxes in them.

The place gave her chills so she made a joke. "Hidden treasure?"

The men caught up with them. All four were still there.

"An underground cemetery," Benedek said, not without a twinge of excitement in his voice.

Goose bumps covered her skin. She really hoped he was joking. "But these are not large enough to be coffins." The stone boxes were no bigger than one foot by two feet, tops. Children's coffins? The thought shook her.

"In the Middle Ages, there was a secret sect that used part of the catacombs. When a member died, they were buried in a regular cemetery to preserve their secret. In a year's time, the members of the sect would retrieve the bones in the middle of the night and would bring them to their underground burial places where they laid them to rest again with their own rituals," he explained, the coffins the focus of his attention.

She stepped away from the wall. "Okay, I'm officially creeped out. The spook factor has just tripled. Anyone else feeling that?"

The guards didn't look affected either way.

Benedek didn't seem bothered either. He looked like he was counting the coffins. "Only two of these have ever been found and both have been looted." Excitement was evident in his voice. He stepped up to one crevice and ran a finger down the stone.

As he adjusted his flashlight, she could make out some carvings before he moved the light again. Looked like an odd sort of writing she'd never seen before. "Secret Medieval messages?"

He glanced to the royal guard and hesitated before he said, "Newer than that. Written about two hundred years ago." He wouldn't elaborate further. Instead, he traced the carvings with his finger again.

"You're not going to open one of those right now, are you?" She was ready to move on. The sooner, the better.

He stepped away and turned to flash her a smile. "As you wish." He wiped his hand on his pants. His dashing tuxedo was pretty much ruined already.

They left the underground burial site and moved forward in the tunnel, which came to a Y again. And again, they went right. This had been their method since the beginning. If there was a choice, take the path that led up. If they were even, take the one on the right. Benedek figured the palace was that direction, and their hope was that these tunnels somehow connected to the vast catacomb system under the palace.

Having a method also meant that they could turn around if they hit a dead end and always know which way to go back.

She trudged forward behind Benedek. She didn't have her watch on, had no idea how long they'd been down here, but estimated a couple of hours. They had walked miles and miles, but due to the winding nature of the tunnels, it was possible that they were nowhere in the vicinity of the palace yet.

She was about to ask Benedek if he had a reasonable guess about how far they might be, when something caught her attention up ahead. "Stop."

Benedek halted immediately. The rest of the men did the same behind them.

She listened.

The men waited.

"I think I hear water," she said at last.

They started up again, and after a hundred feet or so, they reached a section where the tunnel wall had been cracked. A small stream flowed from a gap above, forming a pool in their path. The floor probably had another hole where the water drained even lower down. At one point, there must have been more water, because the hole in the ceiling was sizable.

"You think it might lead to the surface, Your Highness?" Dezso eyed the crack.

"Could be water from Liberty Creek," Vilmos observed.

"Which would mean that we're somewhere near Liberty Park, heading away from the palace." Benedek shone the light above him.

"I could go up and look," Dezso offered. "We could be ten or twenty meters under the surface or closer."

The other guards immediately stood together and held out their hands for Dezso to step into. He went up, standing on their shoulders next.

"Step back." Benedek pulled her away. "Try not to touch anything. We don't need a collapse."

She watched, holding her breath as the man extended the flashlight into the crack, then stuck his head in. If only it could be that easy. If they could all climb up there and reach the surface.

"Anything?" Vilmos asked.

"The path the water follows isn't straight. I can only see two feet ahead. Not enough room to squeeze up there either." Dezso pulled back and thumped to the ground next to the other men, his uniform coat wet.

"We'll drink, then move on," Benedek said.

The fresh, cold water tasted like heaven. She even washed her face free of the full opera makeup. Benedek was right behind her when she stood up, closer than she'd thought. She stepped back too quickly, nearly losing her balance.

He caught her. "You missed a spot." He rubbed his thumb across her cheekbone, beneath her right eye.

Heat immediately bloomed between them.

He wouldn't kiss her in front of his men, would he? He sure looked like he might.

Heaven help her.

His thumb moved down toward her mouth. Her skin tingled in its wake.

She immediately felt aroused every time they touched. She wasn't like this, normally, with other men. She didn't want to be like this with him.

"Thanks." She swallowed and put a more comfortable distance between them.

The guards had already waded through the pool, which was about ten feet wide and hit them midcalf. But before she had a chance to step into it, Benedek was there, sweeping her up into his arms.

"Hang on."

So much for keeping her distance. She had no choice but to put her arms around his neck. "Really, it's not necessary." Not smart. Not safe, probably, not when her body heated everywhere they touched. She so did not need to spend time in the prince's arms.

He flashed her a roguish grin. "Don't let it be said that in Valtria chivalry is dead."

He carried her through the puddle and a few feet beyond before he set her on her feet. For reasons unknown to her, she didn't immediately step away.

The four guards had walked ahead to investigate and were blocked by the next turn in the tunnel.

Benedek turned so he'd be facing the section of the tunnel they'd just left. Probably to keep an eye out for anyone who might be sneaking up behind them.

She found it impossible to relax. The heat and awareness had not diminished in the slightest between them. Just the opposite, in fact.

Especially when he gently pushed a lock

of hair behind her ear. "I'm afraid your very impressive hairdo is unraveling, Madam." His teasing smile would have made a lesser woman swoon—a woman who didn't have Rayne's history with men.

As it was, she could barely look away from those dark eyes of his. And when she did manage, finally, her gaze immediately slid to his masculine mouth. The mouth that had tested hers before, if only to distract her when he'd pulled the shard from her palm. It had lasted no more than two seconds. Two seconds that wouldn't soon be forgotten. She would have thought she was too smart to be this thoroughly affected by something so inconsequential. But as she remembered the brief kiss, the temperature in the tunnel rose ten degrees.

His fingers lingered on her hair, his knuckles brushing her neck.

Unapologetic desire filled his eyes.

Falling into that would have been so easy. His open need for her was seductive in a way that puzzled her. Normally, she couldn't wait to get away from men who tried to possess her. Benedek was different. A connection existed between them that she couldn't fathom, and couldn't deny either.

It didn't matter. They weren't going down that road. She had to step away and turn before she did something stupid like sway toward him. "No," she said out loud to make sure they were on the same page.

"Soon," he promised.

And the tone in which that single word had been spoken sent a delicious shiver down her spine. She thoroughly resented that.

Definitely time to put some distance between them.

But before she could move, they were interrupted by the returning men.

Vilmos cleared his throat. "No more water, no way out as far as we can tell. Should we consider turning back, Your Highness? You might be safer at the opera. That's where the rescue efforts will be mounted. There you might even be able to negotiate with the rebels."

Benedek moved to the front of their small group once again, taking her hand and drawing her behind him. "Not yet," he told his men.

After a hundred yards or so, they came to a three-way junction. If they hadn't stopped to consider which branch to take, she might not have heard the muffled voices ahead.

Chapter Five

She had excellent hearing, and Benedek was grateful for that. Without her, they might have gone the wrong way, completely missing the men up ahead and the exit. If that was what they'd found at last.

Instinct bade him to proceed carefully.

"Which way do you think they are?" he whispered his question.

Rayne took a few steps in each direction, listened, shook her head. "It's almost as if the voices are coming from behind the stone." She pointed at the flat wall in front of her.

Maybe one of the branches looped back that way. The only way to find which one was to try all three of them and fast before whoever was there moved on and they lost this chance.

"Whoever it is, approach carefully. Whether we find anything or not, we'll meet back here in half an hour." He pointed at Vilmos and Dezso and sent them into the left tunnel, then sent the other two guys to the right. He and Rayne took the middle.

"Who do you think they are?" she whispered.

"Maybe we are nearing a section of the catacombs that are open to the public. Could be tourists." But he couldn't put the rebels out of his mind either, or the killer who was down in the tunnels with them, although he couldn't see how the guy could have possibly gotten in front of them.

He glanced back. Nothing behind them but darkness.

"Stay silent until we have ID." He could hear the voices a little more distinctly now as they kept moving forward, although he could still make out only a word here and there.

"If it's some macabre burial rite that involves dug-up bones, I'm going to run screaming into the darkness." Rayne stuck close to him.

He bit back a grin, not taking her entirely at her word. He couldn't picture Rayne running screaming from anything. There was that hidden vulnerability in her silver eyes that he would have liked to know more about, but beyond that she was all strength. "I don't think we need to worry much about secret burials, unless we crossed some time portal down here," he whispered.

When they saw light ahead at last, he turned off his own flashlight. They moved forward more slowly, careful where they stepped.

"Lost contact," a familiar voice, but one he couldn't place, said.

"Dead?" another asked.

"Lost contact with our man on the inside, too. What in hell are they doing in there?"

"Maybe they all killed each other."

"Best case scenario," the first man said.

"And our men on the outside?"

"Completely surrounded and outnumbered."

"And nothing to bargain with to give them free passage. I hate to sacrifice them."

"If the operation takes out even that one damned prince, it'll be worth any price we have to pay for it," the familiar voice said.

He wanted to rush forward and discover the identity of the men. But he couldn't risk Rayne's life. Three men talked somewhere ahead of them. And there could be more who simply listened. They could be heavily armed, while he had nothing beyond a handgun and his flashlight.

He signaled to Rayne. *Let's go back.* They would regroup with the others, then he would decide what to do next. The royal guards were armed as well. Someone would stay behind to protect Rayne, while he would confront the men with the help of the others.

The way back was even slower than the way forward. Now that they knew it was the enemy up ahead, they were twice as careful. He tucked the flashlight into his cummerbund so they had to feel their way around in the dark. He didn't want any light to give them away. He kept his right hand on the tunnel wall so he would know when they were back at the junction. With his left, he held Rayne's hand.

She had long fingers that fit snugly as if her hand belonged in his. Piano fingers. She played several instruments rather excellently, although singing was her true talent. But she was not the high-maintenance diva the gossip columns had often accused her of being. She'd held up under these circumstances as well as any of the men. Still, he wouldn't have minded pulling her into his arms to comfort her, given half a chance. Not that she would let him.

Which was going to make things difficult. Because he realized now that he wasn't going to be able to let her just walk out of his life. If he couldn't have her forever, he would take what he could get. He would marry for duty, but he would allow himself this one last folly. Nobody expected him to be celibate until marriage, and he hadn't been.

Those walls she'd built around herself held, but he wasn't the type to back away from a challenge. He would have liked to ask her what it was that made her so wary of men, but making noise was not the smartest thing at the moment. He didn't speak at all until they reached the junction, and then he turned on the flashlight.

"You should sit and rest," he told her. "We'll wait here for the others."

Ten minutes passed in silence.

"Can you hear anything?" Her hearing had proved to be sharper than his own.

She shook her head.

They waited another ten minutes. The half hour they'd agreed upon had passed.

"Do you think they were caught?" Her eyes grew large with worry for the men.

He'd thought about that. "I wouldn't think so. Ours was the tunnel that led to the rebels." He tried to place that familiar voice and was annoyed that he couldn't.

They waited ten more minutes, then ten more after that.

When a full hour passed since they'd last seen the four guards, Benedek stood and extended his hand to Rayne, hating that he had no other choice but to take her into danger. "We have to get going."

"Where?"

"Back to the rebels."

She stiffened. "Couldn't we wait a little longer?"

"We'd be risking the rebels leaving. We have to find them and follow them. They're the only ones who know the way out."

HOURS PASSED AS THEY waited. Men came and went from the underground room the rebels occupied. There had to be another exit as not one stepped into the narrow tunnel where Benedek and Rayne crouched behind a blind turn, listening. Most likely, they were as unaware of the winding passage to the opera house as Benedek had been before that section of the tunnel was blown open.

Rayne shifted, allowing circulation to return to her right leg.

The chatter in the other room was lessening. Within another half hour, it stopped altogether. Benedek's cell phone showed after midnight when he pulled it from his pocket.

"You think they're asleep?" she asked him, keeping her voice to a low whisper.

"There's a good chance." He'd been alert the whole time, inspecting their surroundings thoroughly.

"Why are they down here?"

"Could be where they have some secret bunkers."

"You don't think they're here to look for us?"

"If that were the case, they wouldn't be sleeping. I'd say the rebels haven't breached the opera yet. If they don't know whether or not we've left the building, they wouldn't have alerted their comrades that we might be in the catacombs."

He'd barely moved, unlike her. She had a hard time not fidgeting. Her body ached from their long walk and from sitting on the hard rock or crouching for the last couple of hours. At times her stomach growled so loudly that she thought the men might hear and discover them. She usually didn't eat before her performances and she was way overdue for her supper.

"I'll check it out. You stay here." Benedek stood silently then moved away from her after handing her the flashlight they had turned off to preserve battery power.

Her hand shot out on its own to grab on to his sleeve. They hadn't heard any noise from the back for as long as they'd been here, but the killer could still be somewhere behind them, biding his time. She didn't want to stay alone in the dark.

"Okay?" he whispered the question.

"Yes." But she had a hard time letting his sleeve go. She was glad he couldn't see the cowardly look that must be plain on her face.

"Hey." The next moment she was pulled up and enfolded in strong arms. He held her, her face pressed into the warmth of his neck, his chin on top of her head.

The sense of relief that coursed through her was overpowering. He was warm, solid and strong. He didn't pull away. He was obviously waiting to see if she would.

"I'm scared. A little," she admitted against her will.

"Come up behind me and keep your distance. If anything happens, run back to the junction and hide in one of the other tunnels." He pressed his cell phone into her hand.

"It doesn't work," she reminded him.

"It has a locator. Standard procedure for all members of the royal family. I don't know if it can send a signal from all the way down here, but if it can, they'll find you eventually, no matter how far down they have to dig."

From the fact that he hadn't mentioned it before, she had a feeling that it probably did not transmit from this far down. But he wanted to give her some hope.

And since she needed that hope, she latched on to it.

"Nothing will happen to you and they will find us," she said.

He brushed his lips against hers. She didn't see it coming in the darkness. And frankly, even if she had, she wasn't sure if she would have protested. But she wasn't ready to admit yet that he was wearing her down, so after a second she pulled back.

Then he moved away, walking close to the wall. The dim light that filtered into their tunnel from where the rebels slept illuminated his silhouette. She kept her eyes on him and her ears open, listening for any noise that might betray that someone was coming up behind her. She followed him at a distance.

She held the flashlight so tight that her fingertips were going numb after just a few minutes.

Once, when she thought she might have heard something—hard to hear now from the panicked rush of blood in her ears—she turned back, poising the flashlight to strike. Nothing happened. Not that she could relax even after long seconds ticked by.

Benedek was a few steps in front of her, coming to a stop. He could see into the rebels' room from where he was now. She held her breath.

"Sleeping," he whispered when he came back and together they moved to a safe distance. "They have more than one room. The way out could open from any of them. I think our tunnel loops around. There might be another exit up ahead."

She digested the information. "You mean we should sneak by the rebels?" Her heart lurched. This seemed like a really bad idea. She was an opera singer. She didn't have any cat burglar skills to speak of.

But Benedek seemed adamant. "As quietly as possible."

The rebels had a way out and it had to be somewhere nearby, was the only thought that could make her move forward, toward them. She wished Benedek would take her hand again, but understood that he would need both hands if they were noticed and attacked. He held his gun in his right hand and the turned-off flashlight in the left. She snuck forward quietly behind him, placing each step carefully.

Fear made her lungs work overtime. But when she found herself gasping for air, she used her usual breathing exercises to calm herself. Couldn't afford wheezing with the rebels just a few feet from them. The whole scenario was so improbable she almost felt like she was on stage, acting out a story. Real life, her real life, wasn't like this. What on earth was she doing here?

Trying to survive, she reminded herself, as she very softly took another step forward.

Soon they were close enough to see the men, four of them. One chair, two desks, a couple of stained mattresses on the ground. Other rooms opened off this one, as Benedek had said.

The men slept, none of them armed, but two rifles leaned against the far wall, mean-looking weapons she had trouble taking her eyes off of.

But when Benedek moved forward, she followed. They had only six or seven feet to cross while they were out in the open. She prayed like she'd never prayed before.

Then she spotted a plastic bag full of Valtria's famous rose-hip jelly doughnuts. Saliva gathered in her mouth immediately. Her stomach growled.

She froze. Benedek's dark eyes went almost comically wide as he looked back at her.

One of the men moved in his sleep. She held her breath. Her stomach wasn't *that* loud. Was it? The guy settled down, and she almost breathed easier again when she saw that his feet now leaned on the rifles, which began a slow slide against the wall, toward the ground.

When those crashed…

But Benedek's fingers closed around her wrist and he pulled her forward before she had a chance to panic.

By the time the rifles did crash to the ground, the prince and she were already hidden behind a wall, and not out in the open. One of the men swore. Then silence reigned again.

Her heart drummed inside her rib cage. Close call. She flashed a weak, grateful smile to Benedek. To think that the most she usually had to worry about on opening night was losing her voice or missing a note… After tonight, she was never going to have as much as a tinge of stage fright again.

If they only survived until morning.

They moved forward and reached another room that opened into yet another room at the far end. They listened carefully. She didn't hear anyone breathing in there. Benedek turned on the flashlight.

Storage.

The writing on the crates was in French. She shot a questioning look toward Benedek.

"Ammunition. From the French Foreign Legion." The question in his eyes was clear. How in hell did this get here?

Another door opened in the back of the room. A faint light filtered out from there. Benedek turned off the flashlight again. He probably wanted to go closer and see where the opening led.

They approached it in silence, Benedek first, she on his heels. Another, smaller room to the right was filled with file boxes, the room to the left with the sleeping men. Another tunnel opened directly across from them. Maybe it led to the street.

They didn't have a chance to check it out. They heard voices coming from that direction. Men who would soon wake the others. Benedek looked at her with a chagrined expression as, moving at the same time, they dove among the file boxes.

BENEDEK CROUCHED IN THE CORNER between two stacks of boxes, Rayne sitting behind him with her knees pulled up. He kept an eye on the men through a crack between the boxes. They had some pretty nasty weapons, including AK-47s.

Six men sat or lay around in the other room.

"So are they gonna blow the damn thing or not?" one of them asked.

They'd been idly discussing the destruction of his magnificent opera. The man whose voice he'd thought familiar was no longer among them. Must have left when the new batch arrived.

"Probably." Another guy, so fat that his belly hung off the mattress, shrugged. "We didn't get any of the princes. The least we should do is take out the building. Gotta show that we mean business."

"He said that?" someone else asked.

They'd mentioned some sort of boss from time to time, but never used his name.

"Sure. Then he told me step-by-step what he was gonna do tomorrow and the day after." The first guy guffawed.

"He'll blow it." The fat guy scratched his chest. "Always goin' on about symbolic this and that. He'll blow it and say it's the symbol of the wrath of the people, or whatever."

Benedek's muscles clenched as he waited for the men to fall asleep again. He wished

Rayne, too, could sleep. She needed rest. But he knew even without turning that she was wide awake. Tension radiated off her.

He surveyed the place again, as much as he could without turning around. Definitely not the rebels' headquarters, as he'd originally thought. No computers, no phones, not even electricity down here. The main room was lit by a couple of kerosene lamps. No real stockpile of weapons, save the few for the men's personal use and those boxes of ammunition in the other room.

From the way the men had been talking, it was clear that their leaders were not among them.

Information storage. He looked at the towering file boxes. Maybe if the men fell asleep, he could open one of them. They could contain a list of supporters, records of donations, maps, plans, God only knew what.

His gaze drifted back to the men who'd stopped talking and were nodding off again, if not already sleeping. Then he looked to the stone floor at his feet and the odd carvings that had been so filled with dust that he would have never noticed them had he not been crouching right beside them, with the light of the kerosene lamps coming through a crack just at the right angle.

He waited another twenty minutes before he risked the small noise sitting down would make. Then he ran a finger over the letters that were similar to the ones he'd found in the burial room earlier. The secret writing of the Brotherhood of the Crown.

Not so secret since an obsessed scholar had cracked the code. The man had been Valtria's most famous code cracker during World War II, and he had become bored after all the action was over. Benedek had read his groundbreaking book a couple of times in his teenage years, as had all his brothers. They'd been obsessed with the Brotherhood back then. They'd all learned the secret code and on occasion had used it to communicate to the great annoyance of palace staff who did not enjoy having to remove their fresh messages from the palace hallways.

Rayne stretched her legs. They ended up on either side of his.

"Rest," he breathed the single word.

He had a rough idea now about the way out, having seen new men come in, but the path was completely blocked by sleeping rebels and there was no way to get around them.

One of the men in the other room began to snore.

Rayne shifted behind Benedek, and he turned to look back, finding that she'd shifted forward. Her face was inches from his as she'd been trying to peer over his shoulder.

She had the most amazing lips of any woman he'd ever seen. Her silver eyes looked liquid black in the darkness, fringed by thick, black lashes. As she leaned even more forward, her breasts pressed into his back.

"What's that?" she whispered into his ear, her soft breath tickling him.

And like that, he was as hard as the stone that had garnered her attention. He turned away from her, realizing that his index finger still rested on the carved letters in the floor.

"A two-hundred-year-old message."

"From whom?"

"The Brotherhood of the Crown. A secret society of princes who saved this country a time or two."

Another guy joined the snorefest in the room next to theirs.

Someone rattled the desk. "Shut up, you two," he said, then turned the lights out.

There were a few minutes of silence. Then the snoring started anew. The guy swore again, then turned on some elevator-music.

"They have electricity?" Rayne moved closer, leaning against his back, resting her head on him. The wall was too cold to sleep against.

"Probably a battery-operated CD player." He didn't mind her nearness. They generated a fair amount of heat between them. He remained silent, giving her a chance to rest, but she kept moving every couple of seconds.

"It'd be good if you could sleep." He figured they could talk in whispers now without waking the men.

A moment of silence passed. "I usually sleep with the light on."

Another moment passed before he registered the meaning of her words. He'd never been afraid of the dark, not even as a child, none of his brothers had been. "Darkness was always my friend. My brothers and I had some serious adventures in the palace after the nannies retired for the evening." He reached back for her hands, wrapped her arms around his chest and held them there. "I'm here."

She didn't pull away, but she didn't embrace him either. Then he felt her relax.

"I spent a lot of time alone as a child. My brother didn't come into the picture until I was ten," she said against his back.

"And your parents?" He was familiar with her professional accomplishments, but her private life had always been kept studiously private.

She didn't respond immediately. "I never knew my father."

He rubbed his thumb over the back of her hand.

"My mom wasn't home a lot."

"So who watched you?"

Another stretch of silence. "I watched myself."

Which didn't entirely explain why she would be afraid of the dark. The thoughts that came into his head made his blood run cold. He covered her hands with his. "Has someone hurt you?"

"No, of course not." The response came too quickly.

"I'm a prince. I have resources."

"I'm sure you do. But I'm hardly a damsel in distress."

No, she wasn't. Not even in this situation. She took the turn of events with a calm maturity and strength. They were in this together. As much as he wanted to, he wasn't exactly protecting and saving her.

"Too bad. I'd like to dash to the rescue, then claim my prize," he teased in an effort to relax her.

"I always knew all those princely rescues were just a means to an end."

"You bet." He grinned to himself. "I wish I could save you from the darkness, but it's too risky to turn on the flashlight."

"I'm fine."

Silence stretched between them for a while, before she said, "We didn't always have money to pay bills. There were times when we had no power for months at a time."

Home alone in a dark apartment, probably in the worst part of town—people who couldn't pay the power bill didn't normally live in mansions. The picture was starting to come together.

"That's when I started to sing. Just to hear my own voice. Singing kept me company. I used to sing till I passed out from exhaustion. I didn't even mind when the people in the other apartments banged on the wall. It was the most attention anyone ever paid to me." She caught herself. "Sorry. I'm starting a pity party. I'm tired." She drew a deep breath that pressed her breasts even tighter against his back.

He'd been acutely aware that she wasn't wearing a bra. The image of that palace photo on her T-shirt stretched across her breasts was burned into his brain. One of her nipples protruded right in his bedroom window, the other in the library.

Damn—the library of all places. Just thinking of it had the power to make him horny. The library was where, at age fourteen, a maid had asked him if he wanted to see her bare breasts. Of course, with time, that led to other things... He'd been a very inquisitive and adventurous young prince.

He found it difficult to think that far back when Rayne's soft body was pressed to his. Now if Rayne wanted to show him something... He shifted. He needed to get his mind away from things that weren't going to happen tonight for sure.

He forced his thoughts back to what they

were talking about. "I thought you were discovered young?" He'd pictured her youth spent in fame and fortune similar to his own.

"At nine. A lot of things can happen to a little girl before the age of nine." There was a catch in her voice.

A long moment passed while he digested that.

He was going to have to kill someone. There it was. He'd killed in battle, in the rebel uprising last year, but that didn't come from a calculated decision. That thought and feeling was new to him, and the sure knowledge that he could be capable of it took him by surprise.

He would know what happened. He would have names. Then he would take care of it. As soon as they got out of here. But now was not the time to push her further into her dark memories. This was the time to comfort her.

He turned as much as he could, scooped her up and tried to pull her over. She resisted.

"See that black plastic box with the holes in it over there?"

"What's that?"

"A rat trap."

She was sitting on his lap the next

second, her feet pulled up, her arms around his neck. She glared through the darkness. "You play dirty."

"True, but don't you feel better?" He folded his arms securely around her. He shuffled back until he could lean against the wall. "I'll watch you sleep. Relax."

The rebels in the other room were snoring up a storm. The sound echoed in the catacombs, along with the music. Those guys were dead to the world for now. He and Rayne could afford to relax for a minute.

She let out a low, ironic chuckle. "I'm sitting on a prince's lap."

Yeah, he was pretty aware of that. Enjoying it. But they *were* cramped. "Not enough room?"

"Plenty of room. Just having trouble with relaxing."

"I'm relaxed," he lied through his teeth.

"Incorrigible."

"On the contrary. I'm the youngest prince. Compared to some of my brothers, I'm all innocence. Butter would not melt in my mouth, in fact."

"Does anyone ever fall for that?"

"Are you falling for it?"

"Please."

"One of the things I like about you is that you're an exceedingly intelligent woman."

She stiffened and drew away a little.

"You had to know that I liked you."

She pulled away some more. "I'm not that kind of a singer."

"I never assumed you were."

"Your attention is flattering, but—"

"Not that," he cut her off. "I don't want the form letter."

"I've had a couple of bad relationships. I had a bad marriage."

"Not with me."

She shifted. "Prince takes singer as lover. Isn't that a cliché?"

"I haven't taken you as a lover yet," he reminded her darkly.

"So you meant you like me as a friend?" Her voice had that all-men-want-the-same-thing undertone.

"I want you every way possible, Rayne." And just thinking of having her had the power to make his body respond. Again.

"I'm not Valtrian. I'm divorced. I'm much older than you are. Are you looking for a scandal?"

"All those excuses are inconsequential," he said, while knowing they weren't. A price would have to be paid. And not only by him personally. A scandal in these politically volatile times could shake the monarchy that was shaky enough at the moment. But he had a hard time considering that with Rayne sitting on his lap.

"So you're not going to accept any reasonable objection?"

"Just one."

She waited in silence.

He reached out to cradle her face in his palms, wishing he could see the expression in her eyes. Her catching her breath did give him some clue. He dipped his head to hers and kissed her.

HIS LIPS WERE FIRM, WARM and seeking. The heat that flooded her in response shook her. She'd thought she would have no trouble at all resisting him, and yet here she was, leaning into the kiss, bracing her hands on his wide chest. Just a moment longer. Because it had been a terribly long time since anyone had made her feel this way, if ever.

They were trapped underground with murderers hunting for them. Without him, she would have been freaking out all over the place. If this were to be the last kiss she ever shared with a man, what could a few more seconds hurt?

He coaxed every nerve ending in her body alive by just his lips touching hers. He was gentle but persistent. He was possibly the best kisser in the universe. When he pulled away, she wasn't ready for it yet.

He held her by her shoulders, silently, as if he were waiting for something. What? A response? She couldn't remember what they'd been talking about.

Oh, right. "What's the one reason you would accept for not wanting to go into this madness?" she asked.

"That you don't want me."

Well, she'd fallen for that trap. Couldn't very well claim that, could she, now that she'd kissed him back like a starving woman?

"Nothing to say?"

She had plenty, but raising her voice was out of the question and most of what she wanted to say would have lost half its effectiveness in a whisper. "There's more to life than wanting."

"Not at this moment."

Stubborn. Probably all princes were stubborn. Used to getting what they wanted. No surprise there. "I don't want a high-profile, lurid affair that'll be fodder for the tabloids."

"Tell me what you want."

He was good. Smooth as anything. They'd known each other for a day. She'd been adamant about not becoming another rich man's mistress, and here they were, with him having talked her halfway into it already. She had underestimated him. But maybe he had underestimated her as well.

"You barely know me." It was a perfectly sensible objection. He couldn't argue with that.

"I've followed your career."

She groaned. There was no shortage of fans who thought they knew her intimately just because they'd been to a show and read articles about her in the papers. She'd gotten dozens of marriage offers from them after her divorce had been made public. She had expected a little more from the prince.

She wished she could move away from him, but the space didn't allow for much positioning. "You know nothing about me beyond the media. Why would you think that we would work together?"

"You know nothing about *me* beyond the media. Why would you think that we wouldn't?"

He was infuriatingly good at this.

"It doesn't have to be complicated. It can be simple," he whispered against her cheek.

"Simple how?"

"Like this," he said, and kissed her again.

He really had to stop. She couldn't think when he kept kissing her like that. She realized that he had a point to make, but so did she. He was proving that he could make her want him. She was trying to prove that she could resist. She was failing miserably. She hated to fail.

Trouble was, she liked his kisses more than she hated failure. Which was very, very disconcerting.

She pulled her head back at last, the move necessitating considerable willpower. "It's not the right place or the right time."

"It might be the only time we have. I want you."

She felt that. Hard to miss when she was sitting on his lap. She squirmed. Made the problem worse. Forced herself to sit still as heat washed over her face. "You can't be serious. Right now?"

"Pretty much anytime, anywhere."

She could tell from his voice that he was grinning. She really needed to get off his lap, but there was no place to go. "You can't just spring something like this on a person," she said in a furious whisper. God save her from randy young princes.

"Would you have preferred if I left things unsaid and instead tried to manipulate you into my bed? Maybe bribe you with jewels?"

"Truthfully, no." She actually liked his straightforward manner. And she didn't want to like anything about him. If she were smart, she would have hung on to her initial dislike of him, even if it had been prejudiced and unreasonable. He was driving her crazy.

"So you do like the way I'm handling this?" He slid his arms around her waist.

"No!" She swatted at him, wishing she could raise her voice. Sounding forbidding while having to whisper was no easy task.

"I think you like me." His voice had a smile in it again, and more than a twinge of surprise.

"No!"

He pulled her against him. Heat immediately spread through her body. She needed to resist him.

His large hand ran up her side.

Her breath quickened.

She was doomed.

And he was a first-rate cad. She couldn't believe that he was trying to seduce her under the circumstances, with mortal danger a few feet away. They were in some storage room for heaven's sake, within shouting distance of a band of murderous rebels. And here he was, trying to—

She couldn't believe that she was even considering it.

When he dipped his head, she held her breath.

"You do like me," he whispered. "And I think you want me as much as I want you. You'll have plenty of time to get used to the idea later, when we get out of here," he told her. "We'll have plenty of time to spend together. Now rest."

She waited.

He didn't say anything more.

He didn't *do* anything more.

Oh, for heaven's sake. This was it? He was

telling her to go to sleep right after making her think that he was about to seduce her right here and now?

"Princes," she murmured against his collarbone as she tucked her head under his chin. "You can't make them see reason, you can't shoot them."

A low chuckle shook his impressive chest.

Oh, that he had the gall to laugh at her. "Once we get out of these godforsaken catacombs, I hope never to see you again, *Your Highness*." She added the formality at the end to drive the point home.

"I suppose you could keep your eyes closed, but it won't be as much fun," he responded.

Her head came up, but she couldn't make out the expression on his face. "What are you talking about?"

His arms tightened around her. "As soon as we get out of the catacombs, I'm planning to make love to you, *Madam*."

Chapter Six

Benedek woke to voices in the other room and put his hand over Rayne's mouth before he kissed the tip of her ear to wake her. She'd been soft and yielding in his arms for the few hours that she slept. A shame she wasn't like that when awake. She didn't like to let her defenses down.

She woke and stiffened when she remembered where they were.

"Good morning," he whispered in her ear, and wished the rebels to hell. He wished they could be like this someplace else, alone and away from danger, their bodies molded together.

"Plan B is ready to go," the familiar voice said in the room next to theirs, as if to drive that point home.

"The entrance was found?" another man asked with deference.

Clearly, the other guy was some sort of leader. Trouble was, Benedek couldn't see him at all from where he hid. The Freedom Council had three leaders, identities unknown. All three were rich, possibly leaders of industry, with enough money to finance two rebellions in as many years.

This guy could be one of those three, or someone who reported to them. Someone Benedek had met before. More than once.

If only he could put a face to that voice, he'd have a name.

"An entrance straight into the palace. Five years of hard work, but it's been worth it," the man boasted.

"When?"

"Tomorrow night."

"And the opera?"

"Security forces took back the building, led by the damn princes. And we couldn't get a single one of them. We didn't even get the chance to detonate the last bomb." He sounded mad enough to spit. "We've suffered some losses."

Somber silence followed, even as Benedek's heart lightened.

"What do we need to do next?" another voice asked.

"Make room for more men. We'll be entering the tunnel system and making our way to the palace through here. We'll get Their Highnesses yet."

Benedek pulled back. The palace was about to come under attack, and not only had he no way of warning his family, but Rayne and he were about to be discovered.

He looked through the gap at the men. Even if he could grab two and switch clothes, both his face and Rayne's were instantly recognizable. Everyone knew them; it wasn't as if they could pass for some anonymous rebel.

He waited until the leader came out of the room. With the light behind him, Benedek couldn't see his face. The man walked into one of the tunnel openings. That had to be the one that led above ground. If only there were a way to go after him.

He looked at Rayne in his arms, her eyes still sleepy-soft, a vulnerable curve to her mouth. She hadn't had a chance to put on her armor yet for the day. But she had to and soon.

He came up into a crouch and helped her to do the same. Maybe they *could* go after the guy. It all depended on how soon those extra men would be sent down. Maybe not immediately since the attack was planned for tomorrow night. If they could sneak up somehow... The move was risky, but no riskier than staying down here and waiting to be discovered.

Their only other option was to find the tunnel that led straight to the palace. But since it'd taken the guy five years of concentrated search and a number of men to find it, Benedek wasn't optimistic that he and Rayne would come across it within the next thirty-six hours by accident.

"We have to move," he mouthed to her.

"How?" she mouthed back.

He nodded as he took off his shoes and motioned to her to do the same. Then he signaled her to stay, and picked up his cell phone, the one thing he could sacrifice at the moment. They still had need of the flashlight and the gun. He moved back into the room that held the crates of ammunition, then back into the tunnel they'd come from. He grabbed the phone and used all his cricket skills to pitch it as far as possible, making sure it would smash against the wall and make enough noise.

Which wasn't difficult. The sound echoed in the tunnel.

"What the hell?" Men came running to investigate even as he drew back. "What was that?"

"Is anyone in here?" They ran toward the source of the sound.

He ran back to Rayne and together they darted into the tunnel that he figured would lead them to the surface. They didn't make half as much noise as they would have if they were wearing shoes, but still enough to be heard if someone listened carefully. He counted on the men making enough noise while searching the other tunnel that they wouldn't hear them.

The first three hundred meters went without trouble. Then the tunnel came to a Y. They could only guess which way would lead them out. Following their previous method, they chose the path that led up. The next junction came soon after, a more difficult decision as it was a four-way split with all the branches relatively even.

They wasted a precious minute, which was enough time for someone to catch up with them from behind. The man was running at full speed. Benedek pushed Rayne into the tunnel on the right then pulled into the tunnel on the left. If the man came into the left tunnel, he would take care of the guy without Rayne being in harm's way. If the guy went to the right, Benedek could take him out from behind before he reached Rayne. If he went straight, they could simply wait a minute then follow him without confrontation.

Unfortunately he went to the right.

In his stockinged feet, Benedek dashed behind him and leaped on the man, groaning when they crashed to the ground with a thud. The guy's flashlight went out immediately. For a blind moment, Benedek groped around, then he finally oriented himself and kneeled on the man's right wrist, immobilizing the hand before it went for a weapon. Then he grabbed the man's head from behind and jerked as hard as he could, back and to the left. The man's spine severed with a sickening snap. His head thudded to the floor when Benedek let it go.

"Stay where you are. I'll be there in a second," he called out to Rayne in a whisper.

He could hear her moving in the darkness, and decided to keep that darkness for a while longer. She was better off not seeing this. He felt around for the man's gun and found a pistol tucked into the back of the guy's waistband. He took that and stuck it into his cummerbund, next to the other one, then found his shoes, which he'd dropped before he attacked.

He didn't turn on the flashlight until he'd walked a few steps in Rayne's direction, and even then he made sure he kept it pointing forward.

"Are you hurt?" she asked, and for the first time, she was the one who reached for him.

He badly wanted to savor that moment, but couldn't afford to pause, not for a second. "We have to go." He took her hand and drew her forward.

"You didn't shoot him."

A shot would have echoed in the tunnels, drawing rebels to them. "He's gone. You don't have to worry about him."

Silence was her only response, then a brief squeeze of her hand.

The tunnel led up after a while. They had to be getting close to the surface. He was beginning to feel decidedly optimistic. But then they turned a corner and ran smack dab into a group of armed rebels. The men were standing, silently staring at a crack in the ceiling. Had they been moving forward or talking, Rayne would have heard them.

As they raised their guns, Benedek tossed his flashlight at the men. It'd been in his hands and was his most immediate weapon. "Run!" he yelled to Rayne as he pulled the pistol and began shooting blindly behind himself as he ran after her.

He ran out of bullets pretty quickly in both weapons.

But by then they were at an intersection. Rayne ran into another branch of the tunnel and he followed her, going by the sound of her footsteps. She suddenly stopped. He ran into her.

He steadied her, ignoring that his hands accidentally brushed up against her delicious curves. She was moving forward already again, but carefully this time, not at a run. Boots echoed off tunnel walls behind them.

He trailed a hand on the wall, grateful when they reached another turn so soon. They stepped aside just as someone shined a flashlight down behind them.

"Not this way, but there's a turn ahead."

"Nothing here either."

"Nothing here."

"We'll split up."

Benedek pulled her forward again. While they'd walked, they'd been fine, but now that they were running, his toes were becoming bruised and bloody from the uneven stone floor. He hated to think that Rayne was getting hurt as well. To her credit, she hadn't said a word of complaint and kept up.

"We should stop to rest," he told her when they'd made several turns and could no longer hear anyone running behind them. Looked like they were safe for now.

"No." She kept on, but slowed.

When they found a side tunnel that had collapsed a few feet in, they used that space to relieve themselves, each while the other one stood watch.

"This is just too gross. I pity people who lived before the invention of toilets," she said after they were both done and moving on.

"How are your feet? You must be hurting. Let me carry you awhile."

"Don't get too deep into the whole valiant

prince thing. These are not sissy feet. These feet danced on stage in prop shoes two size too small. They can take a beating."

But not on his watch, dammit. "I apologize. I had very different plans for your visit."

"I bet," she said in a voice full of innuendo.

He smiled into the darkness. "All right, I'll admit it. I had some vague notions of seduction."

"Vague?"

"Very well. Explicit notions."

A good-natured groan came through the darkness from her direction as she kept walking. "I appreciate the honesty and all that, but I really don't need to know any more about this."

"And just when I was warming up to the subject. Are you sure? Because I'd be willing to share some of the details."

"No!" The word came with a charming squeal.

"I'm guessing you've been the object of many attempts at seduction." Jealousy reared its ugly head immediately.

"Too many," she said without humor.

"I thought women liked to be pursued."

"Within reason."

His protective instincts rose again, as they had when she'd talked about her childhood.

As if her thoughts had returned to that conversation as well, she muttered, "I hate all this darkness."

No sooner did she say the words than they turned a corner and saw a dim light up ahead, around the next bend.

She immediately fell silent. They moved ahead slower and even more carefully. The hundred-foot section took them ten minutes to traverse. But when he stuck his head around the next corner to check for the source of light, he found that it wasn't coming from a group of rebels. Early morning light came through an opening, fifty feet or so above them.

"We made it." She stood directly under the light and raised her face to it. The smile on her face was spellbinding, grabbing him by the throat and not letting go. She looked like a mussed angel with her long black hair having tumbled loose, streaming down her delicate shoulders.

Her signature black pearl choker had slid askew at one point, and for the first time, he could see that it hid a long scar. The welt stood in stark contrast to her perfect femininity, and immediately brought his protective instincts into play.

"What's that?" He reached for her shoulders, turning her to him.

Her gaze measured his, and she immediately covered the scar with her hand, even as she pulled away from him. "Nothing." She looked up again into the light.

The scar was jagged enough so he knew it hadn't come from surgery. A dark need pushed him. "What happened?"

She shrugged and looked fully prepared to ignore him as she examined the walls of the well-like hole. Smooth as granite, not a foothold in sight, he noted that, too. The opening was about fifty feet or so up.

"Somebody hurt you." He looked to the delicate hand that hid that scar now, finding he was unable to focus on anything else, even on the way out.

"A long time ago." Her silver eyes begged him not to push.

"Who?" He couldn't help himself.

"I don't even know his name." She turned to him at last, apparently accepting that he was going to be damn stubborn about this. "I told you my mother left me alone a lot. One time a male friend of hers stopped by. He talked me into letting him inside to wait for her."

His fists tightened at his side. He damn well already knew that he was going to hate this story.

"He said he brought her money. He hadn't. He took the TV. Not that we'd watched it in weeks, it was one of those no money for bills times," she said matter-of-factly.

He'd grown up in a palace, so he had trouble putting her words into context, but not the danger she'd been in. "The scar?" He could see her vividly as a little girl, alone in the dark and at the mercy of a bastard. His blood about boiled.

"He wanted more than the TV. He got sick of waiting for my mother. He decided to slap me around for entertainment. He thought my mother might have some emergency stash of booze. He tried to get me to tell him where. When I didn't, he cut my throat with his Buck knife and left me for dead."

He couldn't say anything. The images in his head defied words. Emotions swirled in him, some tender, some had enough rage for murder.

"A neighbor heard all the yelling and came

over to complain. She called the ambulance. The funny thing is," she added in a voice that sounded studiously unaffected, "another millimeter and he would have damaged the vocal cords. I would have never been a singer."

He reached out and pulled her to him roughly, enfolded her in his arms, aware that he wanted to keep her there forever. The thought that something even worse could have happened to her was killing him, which was crazy because what happened was long ago and she'd made it, she was here.

"It's okay," she said.

"Not in a million years." He dipped his head and pressed his lips against the scar, following the long, jagged line. He wished he could make it disappear. He wished he could have protected her. He couldn't then, but he sure could now. He just had to stop getting distracted by her nearness and his need for her. He pulled back and adjusted her black pearl choker over the scar. "Let's get out of here."

A wrought-iron grate covered the opening high above them. He could hear distant sounds coming from there. Cars. All this time, he'd been looking either up or at Rayne. Now he looked down, at the ground by his feet.

There were coins all over the place.

"What's this?" Rayne asked, noticing the money for the first time as well.

"One of the wishing wells. We have seven in the parks that surround the palace."

"So we're close?" Hope filled her voice. She had already put the past away, just like that. It had been carefully tucked back behind one of those impenetrable walls of hers.

Did the fact that she'd allowed him a glimpse mean anything? He wanted very much to explore that subject, but couldn't at the moment.

"We're very close. Let's find a way to get up there and call for help. It shouldn't be too hard. Half the country is looking for us."

"But the wall is too smooth," she said doubtfully.

"Maybe there are some handholds a little higher up. Get on my shoulders."

To her credit, she didn't argue. When he folded his fingers in front of him, she stepped into his hands, then up. She weighed next to nothing. She must have been even slighter as a little girl, with money not being in abundance. That someone would hurt her— He relaxed his stiffening shoulders.

He had to focus on what they were doing right now, right here.

"Anything?" he asked when she was fully standing, supporting herself by bracing a hand against the wall.

"Same. Smooth. Is there a public park up there?"

"Yes."

"People walk dogs early in the morning." Then before he could comment on that, she yelled up, "Help!" Then again and again.

She did have a powerful voice. He added his own. This could be their best chance for getting out of here. The well amplified the sound upward. Down at tunnel level the thick walls would muffle their shouting. Whatever sound did transmit would echo around the many tunnels, making identifying the direction where it came from difficult for the rebels, he hoped.

This wasn't the best possible strategy, but they didn't have much of a choice. They couldn't afford to wait around until someone happened to walk by.

Calling for help was a good plan. Sooner or later, they would have been discovered.

Unfortunately, their enemies were closer

than he'd estimated. And they got there before their would-be rescuers could have.

By the time Benedek heard boots slapping on rock behind them and got Rayne back to the ground, it was too late. The four armed men running toward them were within shooting distance.

THERE WAS ENOUGH LIGHT FROM the top of the wishing well to see. The space was too small to miss. They didn't stand a chance, although Rayne was praying with all her heart for a speedy escape. But for once, they were completely trapped.

Benedek must have come to the same conclusion, because as she watched, he put himself between her and the armed men and raised his hands in the air.

Always, his first instinct was to protect her. It was a new experience, one she wasn't sure what to do with. She'd always made a point of taking care of herself. Still, his words and actions during their mad escape had wormed their way inside her and touched her in a way she couldn't explain to herself.

Nor did she have the time to think about it at the moment. She raised her hands as well.

"Your Highness," one of the men mocked Benedek and prodded him with the barrel of his rifle.

Benedek turned to give her an encouraging look, then moved along as they wanted him to, without rising to the bait.

The rebels wanted him dead, was all she could think.

The bad news was, they were outnumbered four to two, and outgunned as well. The good news was, cell phones didn't work down here. Which meant the rebels couldn't call for reinforcements. And Benedek's shoulders looked way too dejected.

She hadn't known him for long, but she knew he wasn't the type to give up, not this easily. He was planning something even now, she was sure of that. She had to keep her eyes on him and make sure that if he gave any sort of signal, she would be ready. Their lives depended on being able to take advantage of the smallest opportunity.

Which became infinitely more difficult when the rebel behind her grabbed her by the arm and at the next junction shoved her into the right branch of the tunnel, while the rest of the men took Benedek to the left.

Being separated couldn't be a good thing.

Chapter Seven

"Benedek!" She wasn't proud of it, but she did scream his name in sudden panic. After what they'd been through already, being alone in the tunnel with a murderous maniac, with only his flashlight standing between her and complete darkness, was more than she could take. Her famous fortitude was crumbling.

"I'll come for you," Benedek called back, his voice sure and steady.

No he wouldn't. She wanted to trust that promise—trust him—and she almost could, which would have amazed her had she time to think about it. But instinct honed by decades of hard knocks taught her she couldn't leave her life in anyone's hands. If she were to live, she had to find a way to save herself.

Coming to that resolution helped to calm her initial panic. Business as usual then. The hard times were here and she had to find a way out again. The first thing she had to do was take stock of the situation. Which she did. Only one man escorted her, while there were three with Benedek. And being a woman, a singer, she was most likely underestimated.

She had taken self-defense lessons at one point in her life, but she couldn't remember much. She did, however, practice yoga religiously. The *asanas* helped with the stress of performances and the breathing exercises were good for her singing. Yoga was about strength, inner strength as well as physical strength. She reached to that deep core, stepping out of her silk slipper as if by accident. She stumbled.

"Sorry. Just a sec." She bent for the shoe, positioning herself to face the rebel behind her.

As she came up, she aimed with the top of her head for the flashlight and went with her right hand for the rifle. She ignored the pain where the flashlight smacked against her skull just before it flew out of the man's hand and spun on the floor, coming to rest a few feet behind them, shining in the opposite direction.

The element of surprise was on her side. She jumped back as soon as she had a good hold on the weapon, felt around for the trigger and tried to point the barrel in the general direction of the rebel who had both hands on the rifle now, intent on grabbing it away from her. She brought her knee up, straight to where she thought his groin would be. Judging from the deep groan and the fact that he stumbled backward, she had hit her target. She backed away, desperate to put some distance between them, then shot blindly, moving the barrel from side to side.

And she still missed.

He didn't go down. In fact, he was straightening.

She screamed as the man—nothing but a large shadow outlined by the light behind him—lurched toward her.

BENEDEK HEARD THE GUNSHOTS and heard Rayne scream. That pretty much took care of his plan to bide his time until an opportunity presented itself to overcome the men who held him at gunpoint.

He'd been counting on them still wanting

Rayne only as a hostage. But if the bastards decided to hurt her in any way…

He turned and launched himself at the men behind him, not caring about pain or injury. He eliminated one of them almost immediately, breaking the guy's knee backwards as he fell on him and took him to the ground. Benedek managed to grab and bring the others with him, too. And they didn't dare shoot at him while they were all tangled together.

The injured man howled in pain, scampering to get away from the rolling bunch. Benedek's attention had already moved to the other two and getting his hands on a weapon.

He might have won.

But someone came down the corridor and by the time Benedek heard the footsteps it was too late. The newcomer butted him with his rifle right in the back of the head.

He didn't even see who it was. All he saw was darkness.

RAYNE RAN FORWARD IN THE TUNNEL, relieved that no footsteps sounded behind her. That last round must have hit the man. She had to catch up with Benedek before he and the men who held him took too many turns and she got completely lost down here. She was almost as scared of that as she was of the rebels killing the prince.

Because that was the rebels' purpose. She couldn't forget that, not for a second.

She heard noise up ahead, at last.

Only one set of footsteps. Could be that Benedek escaped, too, and was coming for her. Please, dear God, let that be the case. She'd had some time to think about it and she believed now that if he could, he *would* come for her. He'd been nothing but protective toward her from the beginning. She'd just needed to get used to the idea and accept it. He was so much more than another rich guy looking for a trophy date. He was—

"Benedek?" she whispered, and she could see the flashlight of that other person now, a slow-moving shadow behind it. The size and shape looked about right.

"Benedek?" she asked, louder this time.

The man stopped. "Miss Williams?"

The voice was familiar, but she held her rifle ready to shoot as she walked closer. Then she could make out the man at last. One of the guards who'd originally walked into the tunnel system with her and Benedek. Vilmos, if she recalled the name correctly.

"What are you doing here? Where are the others?" Hope leaped with unreasonable speed. If she found the royal guards, they had a pretty good chance of saving the prince.

But Vilmos hung his head, a miserable expression on his face. "All lost. We split up to find the way out and I never saw them again." He looked up. "But I think I found the exit."

"How? Where?"

"I was in the Army for a while back in the day. We did some exercises down here. I recognize this section of the tunnels."

"Thank God." She slung her rifle to her back over her shoulder, beyond ready to get out of here. But they couldn't leave yet. "The rebels have Prince Benedek. They're ahead of us."

"I'll keep you safe and get our prince back, Ma'am. Don't worry. We'll get out," he said.

Yet another offer of help and support. Maybe Benedek was right and she needed to lower her walls a little and give people a chance.

"I'm out of bullets. I've run into a couple of rebels and had to fire my weapon," he said.

"Thank God you made it." The sentiment

was heartfelt, but she didn't hand over her rifle. She'd only had minutes to feel safe and she needed to cling to that a little longer. "This way." She turned left at the junction where Benedek and she had been separated. "If you take your shoes off, we can go faster without them hearing us." The pain of her battered feet was nothing compared to the danger Benedek was in.

They took off their shoes and began running as silently as they were able. When she thought she heard something, she grabbed Vilmos's arm and signaled him to be quiet.

A scraping sound came from somewhere ahead. The sound of something large being dragged.

Her breath caught, her heart about broke. If she was late… She couldn't think about that, nor about why the prince was so impor- tant to her all of a sudden, why she felt a weight inside her chest so heavy she could barely breathe around it.

She moved forward at a slower pace and Vilmos followed. She turned off her flash- light and motioned to Vilmos to do the same. Not a minute too soon. After a few more steps, they could see the light from the men ahead and their dim outlines far ahead in the tunnel. They were dragging someone between them. The body seemed completely lifeless, the legs dragging along the stone as two men held him under the armpits. Benedek.

Her heart lurched, then seemed to stop for a long second.

Vilmos extended his hand toward her silently, his expression urgent.

The rifle.

He had to be a better shot than she was.

She slid the weapon from her shoulder and was about to hand it over when one of the men up ahead turned and spotted them. He shouted in German.

Rayne squeezed the trigger, aiming high, way above Benedek's head. Entirely by accident, she hit one of the men.

The next second Benedek straightened from his prone position and threw himself on the guy closest to him. He kept that one busy, but the third man was now shooting at Rayne.

So she shot back as she ran forward. Vilmos grabbed her to hold her back, keep her safe, but she couldn't have stopped even if she wanted to. A wave of adrenaline pushed her forward. She registered that

Vilmos flattened himself against the wall for safety and stayed put, but she had to keep moving. As bullets kept flying toward her, she squeezed the trigger over and over again and kept running.

When she was close enough, she tossed Benedek the rifle and hit the ground. Just in time. A bullet flew above her head, so close that the wind of it moved her hair.

All flashlights were on the ground now, all the light at ankle level. She could barely see Benedek as he knocked out his man at last and shot the other without a second of hesitation. Then he was at her side, pulling her up.

"Are you hit?" He ran his hands over her, then crushed her into a tight embrace, kissing her forehead with brusque urgency and aiming to kiss lower.

She wanted that so badly that it scared her. So on reflex, she ducked away from him. "Are you hurt?"

He watched her for a second in the dim light, his gaze unreadable. "No."

Thank God. She could have just as easily shot him as she'd shot the rebel. She was a forty-year-old opera singer, not some commando babe. What had she been thinking? Tremors ran through her now that the fight was over.

"Your Highness." Vilmos approached them at a run.

She pulled away from Benedek. She'd nearly forgotten that Vilmos was even there.

"Where were you? Where are the others?" Benedek asked as he stood. He let Rayne go and moved to collect the weapons from the fallen men. Vilmos helped him, arming himself in the process, explaining what had happened since they'd separated.

She picked up the flashlights. She needed the security of light, the more the better. A weapon against the darkness for at least a little while longer. "He knows the way out." She remembered the most important news at last as she pulled her silk slippers from the back of her waistband and put them on.

"Let's go." Benedek grinned, his shoulders relaxing at last. He clapped Vilmos on the shoulder. "You lead the way."

For a moment, the man looked hesitant. Probably worried that he might make a mistake in front of the prince. Probably embarrassed, too, that he'd stayed back while Rayne had run into a hail of bullets.

Rayne gave him an encouraging smile. She'd only run forward because she wasn't disciplined enough to remain still and cool. She'd panicked and run toward the only person she trusted—Benedek. At one point, after they got out, she needed to think about that.

"You know the way. Just lead," she told Vilmos.

He nodded and started out at a good clip suddenly.

"How far?" Benedek asked, keeping close to Rayne.

"Half a mile," Vilmos responded.

"Where does the tunnel lead?"

"Statue of the Fallen Soldier."

That seemed to give Benedek pause. "I never heard of an entrance there."

"It hasn't been used in decades." Vilmos glanced back. "Back in the day, during the Cold War, it was top secret, used for underground military exercises. From what I recall, they thought it was just a few miles of twisting tunnels. I don't think they realized it was connected to the catacombs."

And maybe they weren't back then, Rayne thought. A wall that had collapsed over the past few decades may have made that connection possible.

They weren't running, but walked as fast as possible. She ignored her aching feet and kept up with the men. She was in the middle, Benedek protecting her from behind. She wished he would take her hand again like before, but they all held flashlights and a weapon at the ready.

Vilmos took the twists and turns without hesitation. Not that they got anywhere. Just when she began wondering whether he really knew the way or was just showing off for the prince, they finally came to the end. Unfortunately, the exit was blocked by a steel door, which was guarded by half a dozen rebels.

BENEDEK SHOT IMMEDIATELY AND indiscriminately. Both Rayne and Vilmos hit the ground as soon as he fired the first round, so nothing obstructed his way. They fired from the ground, not hitting much from what he could tell.

The rebels sent back a hail of bullets.

Benedek went down on one knee to present

a smaller target. He was a good shot, had always been a good shot. He and his brothers had practiced almost daily with their father's hunting rifles since they'd been children, holding competitions in the summer.

When all the rebels were down at last, he rushed forward, putting himself between them and Rayne, Vilmos coming up next to him, rifle ready. If any posed further threat, he would take care of that. But as he examined the bodies, it was clear that Benedek's aim had been true.

Vilmos stepped back. "Miss Williams?"

"Fine. Thanks."

Benedek glanced back and saw that she was standing again. He turned his attention to the rebels. He didn't know any of these either. Whoever the man was with that familiar voice he wasn't among them. Four men, all dead. He relaxed his shooting arm. No further danger would be coming from these men.

Peril came from behind him instead.

"Benedek!" Rayne shouted at the same time Vilmos said, "Drop your weapon, Your Highness."

He spun around, bringing his weapon up, his body going rigid at the sight that greeted him.

Vilmos held his gun to Rayne's head. He must have taken her by surprise, because she hadn't even had time to slip her rifle off her shoulder.

Benedek's blood ran cold. The rebels' inside man had been a royal guard. Dammit, he should have figured this out earlier. Betrayal tasted bitter in the back of his throat. "Think about this," he warned the man.

But Vilmos looked grim and set on his path.

All those men who'd turned up dead in the opera house... Vilmos had access to all of them. A royal guard. "Why?"

"I don't want to retire to a hovel, having to count out money for my dinner." He sneered. "A concern you wouldn't understand."

Maybe he was right about that. But Vilmos had been paid an honest wage for less-than-honest work. There were other ways to improve his finances, if he wasn't satisfied, besides treason. But this wasn't the time for

Benedek to point that out. "If it's about money…"

"Too late to negotiate, Your Highness. I have to ask you to drop your weapon." He kept his rifle pressed against the back of Rayne's head.

Benedek tossed his gun to the ground. "You need only me. She's just been a tool from the very beginning. She's been through enough. She's nothing to you. Let her go and you'll have me to do with as you please."

"I'm more comfortable with not leaving witnesses."

"Then why did you save her?" She'd been carried off by one of the rebels, then came back with Vilmos.

The man laughed. "She saved herself. Another reason I'm not about to turn my back to the American vixen."

Benedek looked at her. He shouldn't have been surprised. She saved herself then came for him, beating him to the punch. He'd been just coming to, making a plan to get away from the rebels and go find her. But she'd gotten free first. And somewhere along the way, Vilmos ran into her. The thought that he could have killed her then and there sent a chill through Benedek. Thank God, since Vilmos wanted to know which way Benedek had been taken, probably to hook up with his buddies, he had to keep Rayne a little longer.

"Take off your tie," the bastard ordered.

Benedek obeyed.

"Put your hands behind your back."

Again, he did as he'd been asked.

Vilmos took Rayne's rifle, then handed her the flashlight. "Hold that." He moved to tie Benedek up, but Rayne was faster.

She hit the man with the flashlight, with a resounding thud over the head.

Vilmos went down, firing at Benedek even as he fell.

Benedek dived for the weapon he'd dropped just seconds ago, and fired back.

When Rayne dropped the flashlight, for a terrifying second he thought he'd hit her. "Rayne?" He rushed forward, his heart pounding harder in his chest than his feet on the stone.

"Here." She lifted the light. "Sorry. I'm getting jittery." The circle of light on the ground was trembling.

She was in his arms the next second, of her own will, clinging to him. He held her with his left, keeping the rifle on Vilmos who lay on the ground.

The man was deathly still. Blood spread on the ground under him, a black pool in the dim light. Dead or dying. Benedek waited a long second to make sure he wasn't getting up. As Rayne's soft curves pressed against his side, he could feel no regret for the man who'd nearly killed the both of them. As he walked to the door with Rayne, he had no thought other than that they were about to get out of here.

Of course, the door was locked.

Fortunately, it took only seconds to find the key in one of the fallen men's front pocket. Benedek opened the door carefully, ready to shoot if anyone tried to stop him from leaving the catacombs. But the small glen was empty, nothing but the Statue of the Fallen Soldier in front of them. They were exiting through a maintenance hole below the statue complex.

Rain drizzled over a gray morning. But they were alive, and Rayne continued touching him, still clinging to his side. He grinned up into the miserable sky, then embraced her fully, turning her face up to his.

"Where are we?" She looked like she'd been rolled down some hillside, hair messy, face all smudged. But those full lips had never looked more tempting.

Cars passed outside the park, a few people were walking the grass behind a glen of lilac bushes in the distance. But his attention was on the woman in his arms.

"Heroes' Park. A mile from the palace," he gave his distracted answer. Then he kissed her.

And for the first time, she didn't protest.

She was soft and yielding in his arms as he'd hoped she would be someday, turning his body hard in immediate response. He wanted her with a ferocious need. But she was just coming around. He didn't want to scare her. So he held back, using every ounce of control he possessed. He gentled his kisses to a few exploratory tastes of her full lips, and cursed the circumstances that wouldn't allow him time for a more thorough seduction.

He pulled away reluctantly. "We have to go. But I swear we're going to finish this."

Color tinged her cheeks as she visibly pulled herself together. "Now we ask for help?"

He wished the solution to their problems

was that simple. "It would be better to find our own way to the palace. We should keep a low profile as much as we can. We don't know who our enemies are." Vilmos was a pretty good case in point.

He took her hand. Out of every terrible thing that had happened, what he hated the most was that she'd been in danger because of him. She was in the country because of him.

"I'm not going to let anything happen to you," he promised, having no idea how he would accomplish that, only that he would.

The opera was probably surrounded by massive security, and every inch of the building was being searched to find them. The search teams had likely found the tunnel entrance in the basement by now, as well, and had gone in there. But finding anyone in the miles and miles of twisting corridors would be a slow and difficult task, so going back in there made no sense for Benedek and Rayne, especially with the presence of rebels. Their chances were much better on the surface.

She offered him a tentative smile that didn't fool him. She was as aware as he that they were out in the open with no backup and possible secret enemies all around them. Vilmos had been a royal guard and still betrayed them. Were there others like him? They were still far from safety.

Chapter Eight

Luckily, they didn't have to sneak all the way to the palace. They ran into a group of royal guards at the edge of the park and, to Rayne's relief, this batch was loyal to the crown. Apparently, one of Benedek's older brothers had deployed them all over Palace Hill, knowing the catacombs had several entrances in the area. They reacted to the news of Vilmos's betrayal with rage.

They escorted her and the prince to the palace under full guard in an armored car. Unfortunately, as soon as they got there, Rayne was separated from Benedek.

She was shown to an opulent suite with two maids at her immediate disposal. They offered her clean clothes and a bath. She would have preferred to go back to her hotel for her own things, but decided that freshening up wouldn't hurt. She was filthy and bedraggled.

She allowed the young women to fill the tub and scent the water with rose petals. She drew the line at letting them assist once she was in her bath. In fact, she asked them to leave her alone for the next hour, promising to ring if she needed them.

Not that they could take a hint. She could hear at least one of them outside her bathroom, probably fluffing her pillows. She stretched out in the giant claw-foot tub, luxuriating in the hot, scented water that lapped her skin, rose petals circling her breasts.

Now that she was safe, their ordeal over, her thoughts kept circling back to Benedek. She did not want to want him. He was all wrong for her. They would have made a terrible, scandalous couple. Which didn't keep her body from heating as his dark gaze floated through her mind. Just thinking of his sensuous mouth slanted over hers hardened her nipples.

He'd be back. He'd promised he would. The things he'd said…

As soon as we get out of the catacombs, I'm planning to make love to you.

A delicious tingle ran across her skin. Her

limbs felt weak, and she had an idea it wasn't just from her long soak in the hot water. Her will to resist him was just as weak. Weaker.

He might not come back.

Except, deep down she knew he would and it filled her with restless anticipation. She wanted to feel his lips on hers again, his hands on her skin... Excitement built inside her already, and for all she knew he wasn't in the same wing of the palace with her.

She was making a fool of herself. She was certainly old enough to know better. She left the tub with a sigh and wrapped herself in a sumptuous robe, then towel-dried her hair. She was finger-combing it as she walked out of the bathroom.

And walked straight into Benedek, who'd apparently been pacing her room. She could have sworn the guest suite had been as large as a ballroom, but the prince's imposing presence had a way of shrinking the space.

Rain beat against the windows, the rapid tapping matching the crazy rhythm of her heart.

I swear we're going to finish this, he'd said earlier. And now he was here.

All of a sudden, she wasn't sure she was

ready for him. In fact, the more she
watched his hungry gaze, the less prepared
she felt. Her hand flew to the robe to hold
it tighter and higher, covering that horrid
old scar on her neck.

He looked her over, head to toe, not
missing an inch, scorching her with his full
attention. "Are you well?"

"Of course." Unless she burst into flames
from the heat that was gathering inside her
under his inspection.

"Maybe Dr. Arynak should check you
out." But he looked like he very much wanted
to be the one doing the checking. "He's the
royal physician."

The last thing she needed after last night
was being poked and prodded by a doctor.
She didn't need medical attention, not unless
acute arousal was a life-threatening afflic-
tion. "No thanks."

His chest rose and fell. He looked like he
wanted to devour her whole, heat boiling in
his dark gaze. But instead of moving
forward, he stepped back. "I brought you
this." He lifted a large royal-blue velvet box
from the antique dresser behind him by the
wall and held it out for her.

Thunder clapped. The air seemed as heavy inside the room as it was outside the tall windows.

She shouldn't have moved closer to him, out of sheer self-preservation, but curiosity had her closing the distance between them and gingerly opening the box. A silver hand mirror with matching hairbrush was nestled inside on a bed of velvet. The royal coat of arms graced the mirror's back.

"My grandmother's. Morin just had it cleaned and polished, and had new bristles put in." He hesitated, watching her face. "Do you like it?"

"I love it, but I can't accept it." The gift was way too extravagant. And she never accepted any gifts from the men who pursued her, on principle.

"Will you toss them like you tossed my roses?" He cocked his head.

Those gorgeous purple rose bouquets he'd sent her before her performances. "I give all my flowers to the staff," she confessed. "I am somewhat allergic to pollen. I have a rule against keeping flowers in my dressing room. I guess I'm paranoid about getting a stuffy nose or having my throat swell up just before a performance."

"My apologies."

"No, it's—" She paused, trying to decide how to explain. "I'm not one for presents."

"You don't want to be beholden," he observed keenly.

"Yes."

"It's yours." He pushed the gift towards her. "No strings attached."

"There are always strings."

"Like with your first manager?"

Damn that he would remember everything she'd told him. "Yes."

"And your husband?"

"How do you…"

"He was a wealthy and powerful man. He invested a lot in your career."

All of which had to be paid back with interest, many times over. Not just in the financial sense. It stunned her that he would understand that.

"I'm not like that, Rayne."

And she was beginning to believe that he wasn't. She hesitated.

"Please." His dark gaze would not release her.

And for the first time, she thought she saw some well-hidden vulnerability in it. Her taking his gift was important to him.

If he'd said, *I insist,* she would have just walked away from him. The quiet request caught her off guard.

"Thank you." She surprised herself by accepting the box and placing it on her nightstand.

"You do need to brush your hair anyway." His gaze warmed, a slight smile playing above his lips.

Right. She did need to take care of her unruly hair before it dried like this. She might frighten the staff. If she walked back into the bathroom to finish her toilet, it would put some distance between them.

Dry hair.

Put on underwear.

Which waited for her on the bed, along with some beautiful clothes in her exact size, domestic magic by the maids.

She was acutely aware that she was naked under the robe, and Benedek was only an arm's length from her. From the fire in his eyes, her lack of clothing had definitely come to his attention as well. He was such a man for detail. She appreciated that quality in people normally, but right now, she wished he were the more absentminded type who wouldn't have noticed that wisp of lace underwear laid out for her on the bed.

Judging from the bulge in his pants, he had.

His immediate response to her was disconcerting. He'd acted the same way in the catacombs. They'd brushed against each other enough times in the dark for her to have felt his unapologetic need for her. It turned her on and scared her at the same time. And surprised her. It had never been like that with Philip. His infrequent trips to her bedroom had always been about domination, about exercising his rights.

Benedek wanted her. All the time. Unabashed. He'd never been less than honest about it. She'd never been less than honest about the fact that it annoyed her.

And he must have recalled that because he turned away, took a few steps back, turned to her again. "Also, I wanted to let you know that the rebels in the catacombs have been rounded up and placed under arrest. The palace is safe. All entrances are sealed. Nobody goes in or out except by royal order.

You're safe here." He shoved his hands into his pockets. "But I understand if you want to leave immediately." He waited.

She didn't say anything. She had planned on catching the first flight out. God, she hated flying. And she would be flying all alone. Craig wouldn't be going home with her. She hadn't even begun to process that yet, although she had placed a call to the agency as soon as she'd arrived at the palace.

"I can't tell you that if you stay a few days, we can have the opening night…" His handsome face darkened.

The opera house was his baby. The damage to that must have gotten to him more than anyone suspected. But there'd be no opening night, not for weeks or months. The two bombs that had been set off inside the building had done considerable damage. She'd seen that firsthand.

"I'd like you to stay anyway," he finished, his gaze challenging her.

She thought for a moment. "It's not like I'm looking forward to flying right now," she said, more to herself than to him. She could have used some time to calm down after all the excitement.

He nodded. He knew. Of course, he knew. No matter how good her PR agency worked, probably everyone knew about her freakish fears and panic attacks.

"I'm—doing better with that." She hated how defensive she sounded. People who always insisted they were better usually weren't. He probably knew that, too.

"A lot of people are scared of flying and you have more reason than most." He sounded understanding.

Still, she was less than thrilled with the discussion. She had made it a point to become a strong woman. She abhorred her own weaknesses.

"It was a long time ago." She sat on the edge of the bed.

He took a few steps toward her. "You lost your mother and brother in a plane accident."

Not a day had passed since that she hadn't thought about it. "Craig saved my life," she said at last. "He held me back from going to the airport to have a vocal cord injury dealt with. He forbade me to wait until I got home. I was pretty mad at him." He'd treated her like a child that night, and it rankled. If she could have raised her voice, they would have had a shouting match right at the hospital.

"Were you close to your brother?" he asked.

This was a topic she'd never discussed with anyone. "Yes." No need to get any more personal than that. Except that the warmth in Benedek's eyes got to her. "He wasn't my brother."

She'd never told that to anyone. And she shouldn't have said those words now. Her life was forever fodder for the tabloids.

"Just between the two of us," she added, and could tell from Benedek's quick blink that she'd offended him.

He was a prince. Did she really think that he was going to run to the papers with the news? She didn't know what to think about anything. She was too tired and he was too close. His strong presence drew her like a magnet. She wanted nothing more than to rest her head against his wide shoulders.

Did that mean that she was weak? As weak as her mother had been?

"I think my walls are crumbling," she said at long last, the fight leaving her all of a sudden.

He took another step closer. "Good. I

want to see what's inside. I want what's inside, Rayne."

She gave a quick, desperate laugh, pulling her robe tighter. "You know what's inside? Nothing. The walls are all there is."

"I don't believe that." He was standing right in front of her now, reaching for her hands.

She pulled them away from him. "The inside is hollow. The strength is in the walls. There's nothing inside but fear and dark dreams and loneliness." She'd never opened up this much to anyone before and it terrified her. She hadn't lied. Her walls were coming down, at least as far as he was concerned. But what if he saw that hollow core and he turned and walked away?

"You're wrong about that." He took her hands again and this time he didn't let go when she tugged. "There's incredible strength and beauty inside. I'm not going to quit until I've shown you that."

Something about that pricked her memory. Craig had said something like that once in the past. About her having to let her walls down someday if she wanted to be truly free. "Craig…" she started, but wasn't sure how to finish as a new wave of grief hit her.

His gaze grew unreadable. "You loved him." His fingers tightened on hers, not enough to hurt, but enough to hold her securely.

She nodded. "I cared for him. And he cared for me, but I couldn't trust that enough to fully accept it. I didn't realize how genuinely he cared for me until after he was dead. He was a true friend. I missed out on that."

"A friend?" His gaze lightened.

"I didn't know. He was on my payroll. You know what I mean? We got along great, but— How do you know when someone really cares? I didn't know until he stayed behind in the opera house because I was there. He could have left with the audience. He would still be alive."

"He was a brave and loyal man," Benedek said.

"I have a hard time believing in people."

"Nobody can blame you, considering your past."

He didn't know the half of it. "My first manager made me his lover. Made me think I was in love with him."

An eyebrow slid up his forehead. "I thought you were fairly young when you had your first manager?"

Way too young to know what she was doing, for sure. In hindsight, she knew now that Preston had simply seduced her to tie her more completely to him. She had been his golden ticket.

Thunder stole across Benedek's face at the same time as thunder clapped outside. "What did that bastard—"

"Then when I was almost twenty, a record label investor came into the studio," she cut him off, not wanting to dwell on the confusion of her adolescence. "Philip. He was even more powerful than my manager. He said he was going to save me. I let him."

Except that her marriage to Philip hadn't saved her. It put her under Philip's control, her and the increasing amounts of money she eventually made. But she found her true strength under that tyranny. And then she divorced him. And she had not been able to trust or love since.

"So there's a reason why you dislike men with any sort of power," he said with a rueful smile, loosening his hold on her but not letting her go. "Would it help if I abdicated?"

She shook her head.

"So you're prepared to dislike me no matter what I do?" He watched her.

"No. I mean, I like you already. You don't have to abdicate."

He gave her a smile of utter masculine pleasure.

He was breathtaking, no two ways about that.

"Preston and Philip were…" She didn't want to stop talking, because she was afraid that if she did, he would kiss her. And she knew she would be lost then. "It wasn't just me. My brother and mother depended on me. We weren't close like normal people, but they were the closest I ever got to anyone."

"And then they died in that accident." His gaze slid to the bed for a second before it settled back on her.

She knew he wanted to sit there next to her, but he was waiting for some sort of a sign that it was okay with her. She couldn't, not even if all he wanted was to comfort her. She wasn't ready, or maybe she was more than ready. Maybe she didn't trust herself that they would stop at comfort. Maybe she didn't want to stop. And that scared her.

"So how did your brother come into your life? You said he wasn't there from the beginning," he prodded her.

She didn't want to talk about it. Which made it all the more strange that words were coming out of her mouth, like a jammed-up creek breaking loose all of a sudden. "At one of the buildings where we stayed, a prostitute lived in the apartment next to ours. During the day, my mother was gone, looking for work or doing this and that for money, sometimes waiting tables in various dives in the neighborhood. Billy's mother slept during the day, entertained her male clients at night. Sometimes, we talked. Then his mother went out one night, trolling the streets for a John. And she never came back."

That had scared her more than it had scared Billy, who'd been three years younger than she. It was the first time she realized that could happen to her, too. She'd spent nights lying awake, worrying what would happen to her if her mother didn't come back one day. One of the many shrinks she'd seen since told her that could be the root of her phobias—all that childhood anxiety.

Whatever infrequent groceries her mother brought home, Rayne had been careful to share with Billy. The kid survived for three months on that. Then one day, a John who was visiting another "lady" across the hall heard Rayne sing. He owned a joint. He offered her money to sing there one night a week. Her mother would have let her do anything for money. She wasn't a bad mother, although she drank more than was healthy for sure. Times were just that desperate.

"I was discovered at about that time. One gig led to another. When we moved, I insisted we take Billy with us." And as long as she brought in the dough, her mother wouldn't ever say no to her.

Eventually she changed. She laid off the booze and did the best she could to make up for their beginnings. Billy had grown into a decent young man who ended up handling Rayne's accounts and doing it well. But there were emotional gaps that wouldn't have been there with a normal family. They all had attachment issues. And despite all of that, she loved them.

"And then they died because of a computer error, a miscalculation of the amount of fuel their plane needed to get from New York to Washington, D.C. The plane crashed two miles from the runway." Her lips were so tight the last few words could barely clear it.

"It wasn't your fault."

He wasn't the first person to tell her that. Hell, she'd paid two hundred dollars an hour to her last shrink to assure her of the same thing.

"They were in New York because of me."

"If it weren't for you, how long do you think Billy would have made it in the first place?"

She didn't want to think about it. God, she was so tired of thinking about all of it, of the picture of the burning plane that was splashed all over the front pages of every major newspaper the next day. She wanted oblivion, if only for a few minutes. So she pushed away from the bed, walked into Benedek's arms and kissed him.

She'd expected a tender response. Instead, he kissed her with full-on passion, and it turned out that was exactly what she needed. Thirty seconds later, she barely remembered where she was, let alone the past. In another thirty seconds, she was naked.

He picked her up to take her those two steps to the king-size bed, lay her on the silk cover. Her body sank into the soft bedding. Before her bath, she couldn't wait to get back here, figured she'd be asleep as soon as her head touched the pillow. Now sleep was the furthest thing from her mind.

His hard, muscled body covered her like a shield. Fire spread in her veins as his tongue danced with hers. Need met equal need.

It'd been a long time since she'd had a lover. Relationships were the one area in her life where she consistently failed. So she'd been alone, a lot. Her body didn't waste any time now reminding her of what she'd been missing.

Her being naked and him fully dressed added another level of delicious tension. At another time, with another man, she might have felt at a disadvantage. Not with Benedek. Not when his dark gaze devoured her.

His clever, all-knowing architect hands explored her body. When his palms came up to cover her breasts, she closed her eyes on a sigh. His thumbs teased her nipples into distended peaks, generating electric charges that ran straight to the heat that gathered between her legs.

She reached up to push off his suit jacket. He helped. She made quick work of his tie and tossed it aside without looking to see where it fell. Then she went for his blue satin shirt, then her hands were spread over his warm muscles. Heaven.

His body had a sinuous strength that didn't surprise her. And man, oh man, was that fancy body doing things to hers that set her head spinning.

He took care of the rest of his clothes. And finally they were both completely naked.

He'd showered, too, while he'd been gone, and his warm skin had that faint masculine soapy scent that got to her on the most basic, primal level. At this moment he wasn't a prince, he was just a man, a man very much aroused. And her body was beyond ready for him.

But, of course, he would make her wait.

He decided to cover her neck and breasts with kisses. Since he seemed to know his way around her body better than she did, she relaxed and gave him full possession, unlimited access. She'd been half dead when she'd climbed into that tub, but now she felt fully alive, energy running through her system.

"I like this spot." He kissed the underside of her right breast.

She liked what he was doing to it. As fantastic as he'd been with firearms in the tunnels, she was beginning to think that his tongue was his most formidable weapon. "Mmm."

"And this." He moved to the other breast.

Pleasure shot through her as his insistent lips found her nipple. She arched her back. Her hands went to his back to pull him up, her knees bending. She almost had him where she wanted him.

But he just chuckled at her.

She hated that he still had the wherewithal to laugh. The best she could do was make those pitiful, deep moans that proved her complete capitulation.

Instead of moving his lips to hers, he moved them lower. What he did to her belly button was pure torture. Pleasure held her immobile. And then he moved even lower.

At this point, even moaning was beyond her.

Pressure built inside her body with each movement of his mouth combined with his soft caresses, only giving her more passionate attacks. Then it all spiraled out of control, the most amazing climax pulsating through her body, nearly lifting her off the bed.

At which point, she finally found her voice.

It was on about the same volume level as her best opera performances.

Her face was already flushed with heat from pleasure and that flush only deepened. They had to have heard her all the way to the coronation room. "Oh," was all she could sensibly say.

He came up and was grinning at her, a smile of pure male satisfaction. "Nice," he said, grinning some more. If his lips stretched any farther, he was in danger of his teeth falling out of his mouth.

"Sorry." She tried to bury her face in the pillows.

He wouldn't let her. "Don't."

And in the next second he slipped on protection and was pushing inside, stretching her, making her arch her back in blind pleasure all over again. She was so not ready for that.

But, as she'd done many times in her career, she rose to the occasion admirably.

His eyes darkened. He watched her as he moved inside her, possessing her body thoroughly. She gave herself freely, moving her hips, caressing him everywhere that she could reach him.

He shifted into a deeper thrust. "I'd like to hear you hit that high note again."

"You think there are a few people in the dungeons who didn't hear me the first time?"

He laughed. "We don't have dungeons anymore."

"Then what do you keep in the basement?"

"Wine. Remind me later to have some sent up."

"I don't think I'll remember my own name."

He shifted again, and the sensation stole her breath. "All you need to know is that you're mine," he said.

It was the exact kind of statement that normally scared the spit out of her and would have made her run for the hills. Except, she was pinned to silk sheets at the moment. And that delicious tension was building inside her all over again.

His mastery of her body was complete. Her bones liquefied. Every cell begged for more of him, only for him. As he kept caressing her, her mind soon became too dazed to be concerned over the complete lack of control on her part. The tide that pulled at her was too powerful to fight. So she gave herself over to the pleasure of his hands and mouth.

She'd heard others compare the completion of love to falling over an edge. This time wasn't like that at all for her. It was like a thousand soaring voices rising to the sky in complete harmony.

He held her afterwards, and she let him, although she'd never been one for cuddling. Something had happened here in the prince's silk-covered bed. Something had opened, a place deep inside her that had been locked away long ago came to light.

She nestled her head into the crook of his shoulder and put her hand over his chest, over his thundering heart. He pulled the covers over them, although extra heat was the last thing that she needed. But after a few minutes, she felt herself deliciously melt into their warm cocoon. Just the two of them now. The outside world didn't exist. Didn't matter. The rain drowned out all outside noise, making the illusion perfect.

She didn't know if she should say something. And if so, what? *Wow,* seemed so trite.

He didn't seem to be struggling with any

postcoital awkwardness. His even breathing ruffled her hair.

Fine. If he could pretend that the world outside this room didn't exist, then so could she.

The exhaustion of their lost night of sleep seeped back into her bones. His embrace was so warm and comforting. She stretched fully against him and closed her eyes. *Famous singer becomes lover of young prince.* That was what the headlines were going to say. That was how the world was going to see it.

To hell with the headlines. To hell with the world. For now, she was going to sleep in her prince's arms.

She woke to someone knocking on the door and had no idea how much time had passed.

"Your Highness."

Benedek groaned and pressed a kiss to the top of her head before slipping out of bed. "A moment, Morin," he called out as he slipped into the fluffy bathrobe she'd found in the bathroom.

He went to the door and opened it only a crack. His secretary wouldn't be able to see in. Still, she sank low under the covers. She would have preferred if their secret remained theirs just a little longer. She wanted to soak up the glow of what had just happened between them. Maybe even entertain a few seconds of optimism that it wouldn't all come to a bad end.

"Your Highness, I've been looking everywhere."

"I'm hoping to get some rest. Out of the way. Any news on the rebels?"

Her gaze fell on the silver mirror on the nightstand. It faced down, the elaborate royal crest visible. She had to be crazy to start something with a prince. But maybe all powerful men weren't the same. Maybe her prince was different.

"That problem seems solved, Your Highness."

She only half paid attention to what Morin was saying. Her body still felt sated; her mind still reeled with the implications of what had happened between them.

"I was just talking to your fiancée," Morin went on. "She's the most pleasant young woman, isn't she? Well done, Your Highness. The Queen should be pleased as well. She's exactly the sort of young lady the Queen approves of. Excellently done." The man couldn't have been more effusing had he tried.

She only registered about every other word. Her heart went cold.

"My fiancée…"

"Chancellor Egon told me. I assume your grandmother's silver mirror set is to be a gift for her? If Your Highness had told me sooner, I could have had something engraved…"

Icicles formed in her chest, causing a sharp pain. It hurt to breathe. It hurt to think because every thought was a stab in her chest.

Benedek held up a hand to stop the man. "This can wait. I'll come and find you within the hour."

"Of course, Your Highness. I thought you'd want to discuss—"

Benedek closed the door on the man and slowly turned, his gaze unreadable, his shoulders stiff all of a sudden.

She was already wrapping the sheets around her and escaping the bed.

"I can explain," he said.

"I don't want an explanation."

The silver brush missed his head by an inch as it crashed into the doorframe.

Chapter Nine

She had fire in her silver eyes, her dark hair in a wild tumble over her shoulders, dipping below her waist. She held the sheet around her with her left hand while she searched for something else to throw with her right. She'd never looked more beautiful. Or more homicidal.

She was of the stage, with a high sense of drama and emotions. He really needed to remember that.

"I can explain," Benedek repeated then strode toward her, swearing silently, ducking a pillow.

She grabbed some clothes and slipped by him, into the bathroom. The key clicked in the lock before he caught up with her.

"I don't want an explanation. I want a car to take me to the airport."

He couldn't keep her by force. Not that he didn't want to. "Chancellor Hansen, the previous Chancellor, married Miklos off brilliantly. It restored faith in the royal family and brought people together. Hansen was murdered during a rebel attack. Chancellor Egon took his place." God help them. "He's... He's still trying to cement his position."

Benedek stared at the closed door, wondering if she would understand. "Chancellor Egon thinks that if one marriage raised the royal family's approval rating so much, then five more would be even better." The man tended to think that a string of happy-smiley weddings would make people forget about everything else and solve all the country's problems.

"So you're marrying for the good of the kingdom." Her voice was full of disdain.

"I haven't said I'd marry anyone." But he hadn't said that he wouldn't, either. The issue was complicated, considering the enormous mistake he'd made in the past.

"Your fiancée might be disappointed to hear that."

"Prospective fiancée. There's been no proposal. I don't even know which girl is the final candidate."

The key turned again. The door flew open. She was fully dressed.

He gave a brief thanks to heaven that there had been nothing in the bathroom that could be used as a lethal instrument. Her eyes flashed, her chin in the air as she walked past him. She shook his hand off her shoulder as he tried to stop her.

"What we've done was a mistake. We'll both get over it in no time, I'm sure." Her words were measured. The walls were up full height and then some.

She was hell bent on thinking him a villain, refusing to consider his side. But damned if he would let her go like this. He closed the distance between them in three quick strides by the time she reached the door, and put a hand above her head on that door, trapping her to make her listen. What had happened between them mattered to him. It couldn't continue indefinitely, but neither did it deserve to be discarded at the first misunderstanding.

"The chancellor is looking for prospective brides for the remaining princes."

She held his gaze, outrage still boiling in her silver eyes, her lush mouth set in a tight, disapproving line. She was a passionate woman and that passion now leaned strongly toward murder.

Something had to be wrong with him that he was turned on all over again.

"I knew there were candidates. I've even seen a couple of pictures. But last I knew nothing was decided."

"And you're just going to let someone pick the woman you're going to marry."

"Yes."

"And then you'll magnanimously decide to love her, or is love something that doesn't factor in to the arrangement?"

He'd loved once and it had had disastrous results. Two days ago, he hadn't thought he could love again. But now as he looked into Rayne's eyes, captivated by the swirling energies between them, he said, "We barely know each other." He kept his voice low. "You can't expect me—"

"I never asked for your love," she said hotly and tried to get away from him. "I don't even have time for an affair. I have a career."

Her chin was up, but he caught a note of desperation in her voice.

"Using your career as another wall. How very original."

She tried to squirm away from him.

He wouldn't let her. "I wish I was in the position—"

"Don't do that. Don't pretend that whatever happened here matters." Her eyes threw fire and begged at the same time.

"It matters to me." They had to find a way to discuss this as two civilized people. Even if he didn't want to be civilized at all. He wanted to haul her back to bed and prove to her that what had happened between them had been true and genuine.

Unfortunately, he was a prince and not a caveman. A circumstance he never regretted more than at this moment.

She shoved him.

He didn't budge.

He needed to tell her something that he hadn't spoken of in years and had done his best to forget. It wasn't a part of his life he was proud of. In fact, it had been the worst mistake he'd ever made, a mistake he'd sworn never to repeat as long as he lived.

"I've been in love before. She was a staff member at the palace." An illicit affair that started with a young randy prince and ended with a man in love a couple of years later.

"You got rid of her, too, when she became inconvenient?" She was merciless.

He deserved that. "I promised to marry her."

"Then broke that promise."

"I didn't. Some Cabinet members had a talk with her. They forced her to resign and move away." Not even his brothers knew about this.

"That must have been a relief, others taking care of the dirty work for you. Why don't you call a Cabinet member and have him take me back to my hotel?"

She was pushing him too far.

"Before I could find Anna, when she thought there was no hope, she killed herself."

He watched as the fight went out of Rayne little by little until she slumped against the door, her eyes going huge in her face.

Dark emotions tore him apart. She might as well know the rest of the story.

"She didn't tell anyone before she left, but she was pregnant." He paused for a long second, wrestling with his emotions about the past as well as the present. "So I'm going to follow protocol this time if it kills me. I'm not going to fall in love again with a woman

I can never have. I'm not going to make promises. I'm not going to hurt you."

But as he looked into Rayne's eyes, he had to wonder whether it was already too late.

She was all unreasonable passion. He loved that about her. Among other things. *Love.* A single word that had him pulling back, a word that held him in place as she stepped over the threshold.

He couldn't afford to love her.

He turned to pick up the phone and called a maid. "Miss Williams is on her way downstairs. Please meet her and escort her to the west entrance of the palace." Then he ordered a limo to be waiting for her there by the time she reached the gate. She was to be taken to her hotel, then to the airport as she'd asked. Next—and this hurt more than he cared to admit—he called the royal guard and authorized her departure from the palace.

He was going to let her go. He'd been clear about that from the beginning. He just hadn't expected it to hurt this much.

By the time he looked back at the door, it had closed behind her. She hadn't said goodbye. She hadn't forgiven him.

He should have been relieved. Better to

end things by mutual consent. If she'd tried to make their relationship more than it could be… She could have caused major complications in his life. Better to head off trouble early, before they were in love and could have gotten a lot more seriously hurt. He had to have learned at least that much from the tragedy of Anna's death. Yes, Rayne's leaving was the best possible outcome for everyone.

Then why did he feel as if something new and magnificent inside him was collapsing?

He picked up the silver mirror from the dresser. There was enough pent up tension in him to lock his jaw. He could have hurled that mirror against the wall. He didn't. He'd never been the kind of man who'd been comforted by violence.

Instead, he set the mirror down and dressed. When his toe caught on something, he bent to pick up the sheerest piece of feminine underwear he'd ever seen. It brought back the sharp pleasure of their lovemaking in a flash. He crushed the soft cloth into his pocket, then called the Chancellor to meet him in his office in five minutes. Obviously, they needed to have that talk about the fiancée, and the sooner the better. This time, he would do the right thing, because he'd sworn he would. But damned if he was going to be railroaded into it. He needed to take that matter in hand.

THE STEAM GATHERING INSIDE RAYNE would have been enough to iron all the gowns in her wardrobe.

She had worked incredibly hard to build a reputation as a serious artist. As soon as news of this little affair got out, that would be over. Maids talked. Men bragged. The end.

She had no one else but herself to blame. She'd known better. How on earth had she come to believe she could trust Benedek? She barely knew him. She was too old to be swept off her feet by some senseless rush of immediate attraction, and yet here she was.

Damn.

She followed the maid down hallways and stairs, barely looking at the people they passed. She felt uncomfortable, not having underwear on. She'd been in too much of a rush to get dressed and hadn't stopped to look for it before she'd escaped Benedek. And once she was locked inside that bathroom, she wasn't about to come out before she was fully dressed.

But even with paying attention to nothing else but getting out of the palace as fast as possible, a group of folk dancers caught her eyes. Maybe they were supposed to have been part of the reception last night, then gotten trapped when the palace was sealed. They looked amusing and fierce with their black handlebar mustaches and loose costumes.

They congregated in the corner of some sort of reception room as she passed through. They weren't too friendly for a group of performers. One pointedly turned his back to her. Maybe they blamed her for being stuck in the palace. The reception had been planned in her honor, after all.

Something nagged in the back of her mind, but the vague instinct didn't gel into anything solid. She was tired. She was upset. She needed to get out of here. Rayne focused on that as she followed the maid.

At a twenty-foot ancient oak door, guards stopped them.

"Rayne Williams. Madam has Prince Benedek's permission to leave the palace," the maid said.

One of the guards immediately called to confirm.

Less than a minute passed before she was allowed to pass through. A black stretch limousine waited for her outside. The chauffeur stood at the ready by the door with an umbrella. The storm had passed, but it was still raining.

"Thank you."

"Madam."

He had a mustache, too. It was a style in this country among the older men, she'd noticed. The young ones followed the Western tradition popularized by Hollywood. Blue jeans and T-shirts all the way.

Except that the dancers she'd passed were all pretty young. Although those mustaches were pretty respectable. Too respectable for men that young? Their leader was older, the one who'd turned his back. And as she recalled his face, something clicked.

Vilmos.

She hadn't recognized him immediately through his disguise, but now that she thought about it, she was a hundred percent sure that Vilmos was that man.

Why wasn't he dead?

She spun and left the wide-eyed chauffeur where he stood with the limo door open.

The palace guard, however, blocked her way.

They had to be kidding. "I just came out of there." She pushed forward.

They deftly moved to block her way. "Nobody's to enter without special permission," the taller one informed her.

"Oh, for heaven's sake." She actually stomped her feet. "Call Prince Benedek. Tell him that Rayne Williams wants to get back in."

The guard raised a skeptical eyebrow.

She held up her end of the staring contest, even as the chauffeur dashed after her to hold the umbrella above her head. "It's urgent."

The man lifted the wall phone and called in. The doors were opened the next second.

She ran through, not caring about the water she dragged onto what was probably a priceless carpet, down the long corridor and up the stairs—she wasn't about to wait until they arranged for a maid to escort her. The "folk dancers" were nowhere to be seen.

By the time she reached the main staircase, Benedek was running down, toward her.

"Rayne?"

The sight of him twisted something in her chest. He was a conscienceless bastard with a royal title, she reminded herself and would have reminded him as well, but she didn't have time.

"The rebels are in the palace," she said.

"ARE YOU SURE?" BENEDEK ASKED for the third time, and that was just during the emergency meeting. He'd asked it a few times before he'd called his brothers and the chief of palace security into his office.

"One hundred percent sure. I have a good memory. That's how I remember scores and scores of music." To her credit, Rayne didn't seem intimidated under the focused attention of a roomful of princes.

He liked that. He didn't like, however, some of the unnecessarily close attention two of his brothers, Lazlo and Istvan, were paying her.

"Exactly nine?" Arpad, the crown prince, asked.

"Yes," she answered.

"And we weren't supposed to have any folk performances?" Arpad asked Miklos.

Miklos shook his head. "I double-checked."

"The admittance logs?" Benedek looked around.

"Since we sealed the palace this morning, only a handful of people have been admitted. None of them folk dancers," Miklos said.

"So they'd gotten in some other way," Lazlo summarized, his gaze dancing over Rayne before he shot a questioning look at Benedek.

So what if he was standing closer to her than was absolutely necessary? "The catacombs," Benedek snapped. "It's all connected to the tunnels. That's where we last saw Vilmos."

"The guard at the entrance of the catacombs reported no movement," Miklos reminded them.

"Can he be bought?"

Miklos shook his head. "He's one of my men." His voice was clipped and with reason. There had been some upheaval in his beloved Army the year before, some of the troops switching alliance to a turncoat general. Miklos had taken that betrayal hard.

"Then there's another entrance," Rayne spoke up.

"Impossible," Benedek told her. "The building was thoroughly surveyed. I've been part of it and I can vouch for no other palace entry to the catacombs than the one we all know about."

"A secret tunnel?" Janos asked. "Nobody knew about the walled-off tunnel in the opera's basement either."

Something to think about.

Miklos picked up his cell phone and pushed speed dial. "I want all of the lower levels checked for intruders immediately. Full surveillance. Double the guards down there."

"Speaking of surveillance." Benedek thought for a minute. "Why is there no record of a group of folk dancers entering the palace on any of the security cameras?"

"The lightning knocked out electricity in parts of the palace," Arpad informed them.

The color in Rayne's cheeks rose at the mention of the storm. Benedek couldn't forget what they'd been doing during all that lightning and thunder either. He shifted on his feet as his body tightened. Rayne was studiously examining the blueprints.

"Thirty seconds passed before the generators kicked in. On the before footage, there are no folk dancers. On the after footage, they are standing around in the green salon." Miklos tapped his finger on the desk.

Now they were getting somewhere.

"Maybe it wasn't lightning that knocked out the power." Benedek rifled through the blueprints in front of him and pulled out the one that illustrated the green salon. "So we need to check every spot from where the green salon can be reached within thirty seconds."

He pored over every detail, thinking about every little thing he knew about that part of the palace. The solution seemed too obvious. "The wine cellars?"

Janos, Istvan and Miklos headed off immediately, the chief of palace security right behind them.

Benedek held him back. "Please arrange for an escort to take Miss Williams back to her room. She's to stay there under heavy guard until further notice from me."

He paused on his way to the door and took in the wide-eyed, dismayed expression on her face, hating to let her out of his sight. Then he sprinted after Arpad, who as Crown Prince should have been staying out of all possible trouble instead of running off to find some secret catacomb entrance to the palace.

Chapter Ten

Benedek caught up with the others just as Miklos was handing out weapons from the armory. Miklos glanced toward another locked cabinet, then back to his brothers with a questioning look.

They were all grinning.

"Hurry," Benedek said and held out his hand, grabbing the sword Miklos pulled from the other cabinet.

When the last brother received his sword, they saluted each other. When the swords were sheathed, Arpad put his hand in the middle. They all followed his example.

"Duty and honor, our lives for the people and the crown," they swore the oath of the Brotherhood of the Crown as one. And then they were running to meet the enemy.

Arpad took the lead, but only for a second.

"Crown Prince to the back!" Miklos cut in front of him. "You need to be protected."

Arpad glared. "It's no fun to be Crown Prince."

"Married man with a baby to the back." Istvan elbowed in front of Miklos.

"I know the palace best." Benedek jockeyed for position. He'd studied every inch of the building while he was completing his education as an architect. Unnamed emotions swirled inside him and pushed him forward. What he had with Rayne was complicated. Fighting the rebels was simpler.

Tension and regrets filled him, pushing him forward, making him anticipate the clash. He would let Rayne go. He would not second-guess that decision. He would make sure the palace was safe, that she was safe. He would not let anything happen to her.

He might even try to talk to her one last time. But he had to let her go in the end.

They passed royal guards on the stairs.

"Give way," Benedek ordered, and the men parted for the princes, then followed behind them.

Shots sounded. Benedek ran faster.

He spotted the rebels coming up on the last set of stairs, which meant that the royal guard who'd been sent to seal the wine cellar had been defeated. From the looks of things, the whole basement level had already been taken over.

Benedek drew his gun. Unfortunately, the royal guard who'd been content to follow until this, now rushed forward to protect the princes, spoiling his fun. Not for long. The rebels outnumbered the defending force, so he had his hands full soon enough.

The rebels were shooting wildly, hardly the trained force the royal guards were. Benedek looked for their leader. If he was eliminated, maybe the rest would pull back. He found the man and aimed, but a chunk of loose stucco fell and clonked Benedek on the shoulder, messing up his shot.

This part of the palace had been built in the eighteenth century. He was more concerned for the building than for the dull pain in his shoulder. Priceless frescoes covered the walls. A firefight here was a crime, a sacrilege. Not that the rebels cared.

First the damage to the opera house and now the fight at the palace, the symbol of the monarchy, the home of his ancestors going back centuries. He took out a tall lumberjack type who'd lunged at Arpad, then yelled over the din, "Gentlemen, watch the architectural features!"

Miklos let out a bark of laugher behind him.

Easy for him—he was an Army major, a warrior, not an architect.

RAYNE HADN'T BEEN IN HER ROOM two minutes before she heard shooting from outside the door. And bodies falling to the floor.

"Is everyone okay out there?"

No response came, except the sound of people running, boots slamming on the antique parquet of the hallway.

A minute passed before she decided to check out what was going on. Then another minute before she found a makeshift weapon, a cast-iron candle holder that was as long as her arm. She spent two minutes trying to get the door open, which, apparently, had been locked from the outside.

"Hey! Anybody out there?"

An acrid smell hit her nose, so faint that seconds passed before it set off the alarms in her brain. Smoke. And then she saw the faint wisps, too, as she looked down. Smoke seeped in under the door, through a narrow gap.

Her heart lurched as she pounded the door with all her strength. "I'm in here. Help!"

No response, not a sound from the hallway.

She was locked in and the palace was on fire.

Where was Benedek? If the palace was on fire, didn't it mean that the rebels had taken over? Could be Benedek was injured or worse. Her heart beat faster.

She coughed, looked up to blink the tears the smoke brought to her eyes, and realized that she could barely see the angels on the ceiling. It would be only a matter of time before the smoke filled the room completely.

"There's no reason to panic," she tried to reassure herself, using the mantra she'd been taught by her second therapist.

Since the smoke was coming from the hall, it meant that the situation would be a lot worse out there. Even if she could somehow break the solid wood door down, she probably couldn't pass that way. Likely, she'd be walking into fire. The only way out of the room was cut off. She was trapped.

"There's no reason to panic." She stepped back.

She didn't want to burn. The news photos of her mother and Billy flashed into her mind, nearly paralyzing her. Flames and smoke. She'd had nightmares about that for years afterwards, dreaming of them trapped in their airplane seats while flames licked at them, screaming for her help. She never could help, not even in her dreams. Instead, she usually woke with a cry, soaked in sweat and guilt. There were variations on the dream. Sometimes she was in the flames with them.

She could feel the heat of the fire outside through the closed door. She glanced toward the bathroom. The tub? Or she could open the shower and stand under the water. But that still wouldn't save her from smoke inhalation.

"There's no reason to—" Who was she kidding? She had plenty of reasons to panic. And if Dr. Andrew was here with her, he'd panic right along with her.

She ran to the window. Maybe she could call for help outside.

But the window looked over a formal garden, evergreens sheared to form sophisticated shapes, a labyrinth with an amazing gazebo in the middle. At another time, she could have appreciated the beauty of it, but all she felt now was desperation that the garden was completely deserted.

"Help!" she tried anyway, yelling into the void. She could see people through other windows, running down hallways.

"Help!" She knew how to make her voice carry.

Unfortunately, it didn't look like anyone heard her.

She looked down at the balcony below her, a twenty-foot drop. Because all the rooms of the palace had to have all these damned high ceilings.

Fire alarms began to go off.

About time. She couldn't imagine what took so long.

Maybe help would come now. But what if it came too late?

She stared at the balcony beneath hers, contemplating a jump. She was a singer and, although she had danced on stage if a particular role called for it, she wasn't athletic. She just wasn't the leaping kind.

She stepped back into the room just as the

sprinklers went off. Within seconds, she felt like a drowned rat, which didn't improve her mood much. But then she considered that maybe the sprinklers were going in the hallway as well. Maybe they were enough to put out the fire.

She ran to the door. The smoke coming in did lessen. She took a few steps back and ran into the door, trying to bust it open. When that didn't work, she tried it with a chair. Nothing budged, so she went back to banging and yelling. "I'm in here! Let me out! I'm in here!"

She was hoarse by the time the key finally turned in the lock and the door opened. Not by Benedek or a royal guard, to her great dismay.

"Where's the prince?" Vilmos pointed a gun right at her heart as he asked.

"I have no idea. Not here."

Vilmos grabbed her by the shoulder and dragged her out into the hall where wallpaper was still burning in places, despite water raining down from above. The walls and carpets were black.

"You're coming with me," he said.

THINGS HAD GONE TOO FAR. There were rebels in the royal palace. For the second time in a year, the monarchy was under attack, the Queen threatened in her own home—his mother who'd spent her entire life serving her people. And she was ill. Too ill to be put through this again.

Benedek held back nothing and neither did his brothers.

The original Brotherhood of the Crown had nothing on them. The six princes fought like a pack of lions, backed up by the royal guard, holding off a much larger force that was trying to make its way up from the basement.

Men had fallen on either side, but none of the princes were injured. Not yet. Although a bullet had ripped Janos's jacket on his shoulder.

They were all insane. If they cared anything about protocol, none of them should be here. But they weren't the ornamental kind of princes that the royal family brought out on public occasions. They each had their indomitable ancestors' blood in them that didn't mind running into a good fight now and then.

They'd even resurrected the Brotherhood of the Crown, two hundred years after the original had been created to fight for the country and the crown. Their mother knew nothing about this. No one outside the brothers did.

Benedek fought back a rebel and jumped to the side to reload when his gun was empty. Some ringing noise came from somewhere above, deep in the palace.

"What's that?" he shouted to one of the royal guards who had an earpiece. Likely, he was in radio contact with central command.

"Fire alarm," Istvan said. He was standing higher up the stairs and could probably hear better.

There could *not* be a fire in the palace. Cold fury filled Benedek. "Where's the fire?" he demanded from the guard.

The man asked over his radio, then said, "East wing. Third floor, Your Highness."

Rayne.

The damage to the opera house and the palace angered him, but he could deal with that. The cold fear that filled him now had almost brought him down, however. He turned to break through the fighting crowd, but a rebel chose that moment to vault on top of him. And he hadn't finished reloading his gun yet. That alarm had distracted him.

This was the exact moment when a sword

came in handy. He pulled the length of tempered steel and saw fear flash in the man's eyes. The bastard hadn't seen anything yet.

Benedek finished his man and reloaded his gun at last. But before he could go to Rayne, another large group of rebels appeared out of nowhere, coming from behind the princes and their faithful guards.

They were surrounded.

RAYNE KICKED AND SCREAMED, BUT Vilmos was much stronger. And he had a gun, which really was the final word in the argument.

The one thing that gave her hope was that Vilmos had asked about Benedek. Which meant that the rebels didn't have him yet.

How important that was surprised her. It seemed impossible that she of the impenetrable walls could come to care this much about a man in such a short time. But her concern for him went way beyond the concern she felt for the rest of the people in the palace. She cared on a deeper level, in a way that squeezed her chest. The thought that something might happen to him scared her more than the fire.

She so did not want to consider the implications. It would be beyond insane to let her guard down and fall in love with a man who had just discarded her. After one encounter of incredible passion. It *had* been incredible. She had to give him that. But probably not incredible enough to make up for all the heartache that was about to hit her.

A door slammed open in front of them. Hope leaped. And was immediately crushed. More rebels were coming up some servants' staircase, ten of them. When they were all up, going about the dark business of completely invading the palace, Vilmos took her down the same staircase. Then down and down and down, passing by a number of exits.

She had a bad feeling about this. "I'm not even Valtrian. I'm not involved in any of this. You could just let me go."

Vilmos laughed darkly. "I might be a generation older, but I'm not blind yet. The young prince would give much for you. You'll make a fine bargaining chip if things come to that."

"The young prince has a fiancée," she snapped. That she would have to be the one to share that piece of *good news* galled beyond words. "Maybe you should be looking her up?"

The information took the man aback, but only for a second. "I have the one he wants," he said, sounding pretty self-assured.

Prince Benedek did not want her beyond a quick conquest, but it was too demoralizing a news flash to share with a conscience-less rebel. "You might be disappointed," was all she said. She certainly had been.

"Insecurity between lovers. Isn't that sweet?" Vilmos mocked her.

She wished they would stop so she could kick him in the shin. But he was pulling her along at a fast pace on narrow stairs. She didn't want to add falling on her face to the list of indignities she'd been given to suffer today. She was in plenty of trouble already. She could do without any broken limbs.

Which gave her an idea.

She hooked her foot in front of Vilmos's the next second.

He did tumble. Unfortunately, he dragged her with him as they rolled down the stairs that seemed a mile long all of a sudden.

"Oh, God." She moaned into the pain.

Her ribs felt like they were going through a meat grinder.

Just when she thought it couldn't get any worse, they slammed against the wall at the bottom, with him on top of her.

For a moment, they were both still. Then he pushed off her with one hand and unceremoniously backhanded her with the other.

"Get up," he yelled.

She did, her cheek stinging, every muscle protesting. They were all the way down at the bottom, in a basement. She hadn't succeeded in holding him back from taking her wherever he wanted. She had simply got them there faster.

Way to go. She could only hope men with better combat skills than she were in charge of defending the palace.

He dragged her across a small room. A boiler room, she realized after a minute. He took her all the way to the back, to a ratty old closet. The key he pulled from his pocket opened the padlock on the door. He shoved her inside and locked the door behind her.

She was all alone in the darkness, locked in a closet. Shelves dug into her back. The smell of chemicals choked her. She tried to shift to get some fresh air through the crack in the door, and pushed against the shelves accidentally. Bottles rattled. The shelves moved back.

Strange.

She pushed back a little more. Once again, the shelves accommodated her. She had enough room now to turn around and push with both hands. The shelves kept going and going. She stopped and felt around in the darkness, drawing back when her fingers got tangled in cobwebs. She could hear nothing but some squeaky noises in the distance, which she hoped to heaven weren't rats.

Because by now she had a pretty good idea that she wasn't inside any cleaning closet. She was back in the catacombs, this time without Benedek. And if anything happened to Vilmos in the fight, nobody would know that she was down here.

Even if Vilmos did come back for her, it would only be to use her against Benedek. She gave a few moments of thought to that. She was mad at him, but not mad enough to want to see him hurt. Her anger had cooled quite a bit, actually, now that she wasn't sure how he fared and whether she would make it out of this place alive.

He was expected to make a royal alliance. All the princes were. He hadn't been engaged, not truly, not yet. He'd said he hadn't even met the girl. He'd just agreed to some vague notion of doing his duty. She'd known going in that anything serious between them would be impossible.

She was as much to blame as he.

She'd been attracted to him. From the beginning. And she'd resented him because of that unwanted attraction. Then they were forced together in close proximity and the attraction grew into full-blown lust. Then she got to know him better and...

She couldn't think about his gentle touch and scorching passion and understated sense of humor, or his courage, the way he risked life and limb to protect her from the rebels. If she contemplated that, she was going to fall headlong in love with him and that would cause nothing but trouble.

Not that she needed to look for more trouble. She faced plenty where she was, right here. The yawning darkness in front of her was a physical presence, like a beast waiting to devour her. Obviously, Vilmos had thought that she would be too scared to venture forth in the darkness and get away from him.

Staying put would have been the smart thing for sure. But what if there was another exit someplace near? If she could only find that, she might be able to get to a section of the palace that wasn't yet controlled by the rebels.

The tunnel was absolutely pitch-dark and moldy. She sneezed. More squeaking from up ahead. Dear God, was she really going to walk toward that? But what other choice did she have?

She hadn't run into any rats in the tunnels with Benedek, but it made sense that there'd be some in the immediate vicinity of the palace where they could get in through the cracks and steal food. Not a theory she wanted to contemplate. She held her hands out in front of her so she wouldn't rush smack into a wall, and moved forward.

Something light ran across her foot in the darkness.

"Shoo!" She just knew it had been a rat. She almost turned back to wait obediently by the door for Vilmos. But then she thought of

Craig. That bastard had already killed her agent. He was not going to get her, not as a pawn and not as a victim. She gathered up her strength and took another step forward into the darkness.

She didn't want to fall for fear of falling on a rat. The thought that they might crawl on her was more than she could bear. Maybe noise would scare them away.

She began to sing. It was just like when she'd been a child, singing to hold the darkness at bay. God, it brought back memories and not the good kind. She'd never thought that one day she'd be back here, scared and all alone.

Except that she wasn't a child anymore with limited options. She was a grown woman. A strong woman. Not just her walls, but on the inside. Wasn't that what Benedek had said?

No wonder she was falling for him.

She couldn't have him. But she could have her life back. Without her paralyzing fears. She'd begun to overcome her fear of flying. She'd made it all the way to Valtria. Maybe next she could let go of her fear of allowing people to get close to her. Even if she did get burned now and then.

Benedek had taught her that. What had happened between her and Benedek still hurt, but did she wish that she hadn't spent those few hours in his arms? Maybe she was crazy and self-destructive, but she didn't.

She sang louder. The aria from *Aida* comforted her somewhat. But instead of the notes, as uplifting as they were, she wished she had Benedek.

Chapter Eleven

At least an hour passed before Benedek could extricate himself from the battle in the basement and go to rescue Rayne. The fire alarms had stopped by then. He ran down the hallway, blocking out the damage, and nearly ran into a rebel. Since he'd completely run out of bullets, he used his sword to dispatch the man.

He heard a noise behind his back, a door opening. He spun, his sword ready.

"Your Highness!" Chancellor Egon was pale and shaking, shrinking back.

"Have you seen Miss Williams?" was Benedek's first question.

"I just came up, looking for you, Your Highness."

Benedek ran forward. "How is the Queen?"

"Safe."

"Keep her that way." The closer he got to Rayne's room, the more charred the carpets and wallpaper were. Her door stood open. He burst into the room. Balcony door open. He checked there. Nothing. Not in the bathroom either.

"Your Highness—"

"You go to central command and let the royal guard know to look for Rayne Williams."

"Your Highness…" The man hesitated, but then barreled forth. "It would not do to have your name associated with Miss Williams. Your fiancée—"

"I don't have a fiancée." Benedek strode out of the room. He had to figure out where Rayne had gone.

"But you had agreed to a royal match." The Chancellor ran behind him.

"And I just changed my mind." He left the Chancellor gaping. The door to the servants' staircase stood open. Maybe Rayne had gone in there.

"But, Your Highness, you've always been the reasonable one, if I might say, not at all like your twin brother—"

"Get word to the royal guard about Miss

Williams. Or you're going to find out just how unreasonable I can get," he ordered, and ran down the stairs.

Trouble was, he had no idea where Rayne might have exited the staircase. He ran out to the second floor. Meeting rooms and a media room, a small movie theater took up most of it in this wing. Not much looked touched here.

"Rayne!"

No response.

"Rayne! It's Benedek." He ran down the hall and opened doors randomly. Nobody there.

He ran back into the staircase, to the first floor. A small fight raged here, one he didn't engage in. "Did you see Miss Williams?" he asked the nearest royal guard, a man who pulled into cover to reload his weapon.

"No, Your Highness."

A rebel rushed at them. Benedek ran him through with his sword before the surprised guard had a chance to get off a shot.

"Thank you, Your Highness." The guard had his gun ready and stepped in front of him.

Benedek backed into the staircase and took the stairs two at a time to the basement level. The boiler room was on the opposite end of the palace from the wine cellar. No rebels down here. Nothing at all.

"Rayne!" he yelled anyway, but received no response. If he were the type to punch holes in walls, this would have been the time. But taking one's frustration out on architectural elements was not his thing. He took the stairs up two at a time, exited on the first floor, dispatched one rebel after another until he found one with a radio.

He grabbed that one by the neck. "Make contact."

"With whom?" The man gasped for air.

"Whoever is in charge here."

The connection crackled to life in a second.

"This is Prince Benedek. I want Rayne Williams," he said into the receiver.

"Meet me in the coronation room," a staticky voice said.

Benedek tossed the receiver at the same time as the rebel went for Benedek's gun. The guy miscalculated, surprise on his face when nothing happened after he pulled the trigger. Benedek cut him down where he stood, then ran for the coronation room, knowing there was a better than good chance that it was a trap.

He encountered sporadic fighting on his way. Everywhere, rebels were winning. There had to be a reason that the Army wasn't here yet. Maybe the Chancellor was wrong and the Queen wasn't safe. Maybe the rebels were holding her hostage, holding the Army at bay with that threat.

Miklos had cleaned the Army of all traitors recently. Benedek couldn't imagine that anyone could turn the current generals against the monarchy.

He slowed as he reached the coronation room. Inspected the hallway. Nobody there. The door was closed. He pushed it open slowly.

Empty.

He wasn't given to foul language, but now he swore under his breath. He walked the perimeter of the room. Maybe something had been left here for him. A clue.

And, yes, it had. Someone had cut letters into the red velvet of the throne itself. HUNTERS' DINING ROOM, the message said.

He ran out the door and down the hallway, down the stairs. The Hunters' Dining Room had been his father's favorite, the king having been a great huntsman. It was the most masculine room in the castle. And often, the only escape for the princes. The ladies of the court hated dinners held here and often excused themselves.

The walls were dark wood, as was the ceiling, the chandeliers made of enormous antlers. The decoration was overwhelmingly dead. Taxidermy reigned free here. Growling bears with five-inch incisors, mountain lions, elk and a list of other trophies stood silently.

Vilmos stepped from behind a richly carved gun cabinet, holding a gun at Benedek.

He'd shot the man in the tunnel. "You were dead. How did you get here?" Benedek kept his sword ready, knowing he could do little against a bullet.

"I guess you missed the important parts. Everyone makes mistakes. Don't be too hard on yourself, Your Highness." Vilmos smiled with a mad fire in his eyes.

He didn't have time for this. He had to find Rayne. "They're using you. Whatever they said you were going to get after you assassinated me and my brothers at the opera, you wouldn't have gotten it. They would have blown the building anyway. They would have killed you," he bluffed.

But Vilmos only laughed. "That was the plan. It's been a suicide mission from the get-go. I volunteered." Hate boiled in his gaze. "I had to make sure that Their Highnesses were in the security office when the big bomb blew right on top of them."

To kill for a cause was one thing, to be willing to die for it took a whole other level of conviction. "Why?" Benedek asked. "What did my family ever do to you?" He no longer bought what Miklos had said before about the money. This felt more personal.

"Killed my sister."

He stared at the man. The guy was crazy.

"Remember Anna?" Vilmos said. "You didn't know, did you? She was my little sister. Different names. We had different fathers. She was young and sweet, an innocent thing before she met you."

Young and sweet but no longer all that innocent. She'd initiated the affair, in fact. The seduction had been rather mutual, but this wasn't the time to mention that. "I never meant for that to happen. I'm sorry about Anna." More sorry than he could ever say.

"I was the only one she told everything to. What could I do? She disgraced herself. The prince's mistress, carrying the prince's bastard. She shouldn't have asked me for help." Vilmos's face was as dark as the catacombs had been.

A hundred questions flew through Benedek's mind, but before he could voice any, Vilmos said, "One prince down, five more to go. How about you go next?"

He glanced to the gun cabinet behind Vilmos. A hunting rifle would have been a great help, but the cabinets were kept locked and he didn't have his key on him at the moment.

One down. That had to mean one of his brothers. His blood ran cold at the prospect, his attention drawn away from Anna and the past. "You lie."

"You didn't feel it? I guess all that talk about a special connection between twins must be a myth then."

"Lazlo is not dead."

"You can check with him in a minute when you're walking the fiery road to hell together."

A bonfire of rage burned in his chest. That the man wouldn't make it out of the dining room was a foregone conclusion. "Where is Rayne?"

"Exactly where I want her to be. And proving extremely useful. Got you here, didn't she?"

Benedek had no choice but to rush the man. With ten meters of distance between them, Vilmos was at an advantage. But in hand-to-hand combat, a sword could be just as dangerous as a gun.

Vilmos knew that. He fired, missing Benedek, but hitting the sword just above its handle. The weapon flew out of Benedek's hand.

He needed five more meters before he could reach Vilmos, and disarm him. The next bullet would end everything.

Except that Vilmos's pistol clicked empty. That was all the break Benedek needed. He grabbed the nearest trophy from the wall above his head and charged at Vilmos with the antlers. He pinned the man against the gun cabinet, the antlers going through flesh.

"Where's Rayne?"

Blood bubbled from between Vilmos's lips. He choked on it as he said, "In the catacombs."

"Where? Which entrance?" He was careful to hold the trophy in place, not wanting to cause more damage for the moment, not until he had the information he needed.

"I'll let you know when we meet in hell." Vilmos thrust his body forward and finished the job, impaling himself completely.

"Where?" Benedek swore and shook him. He pulled the antlers back.

But he was too late. Vilmos was dead.

And Rayne, who was more scared of darkness than anything else in life, was lost somewhere below the palace in a maze of dark tunnels.

BY THE TIME SHE REALIZED THAT there were no other exits nearby and her best chance of rescue was to go back to the door that led to the palace's boiler room, she had taken too many turns and could no longer find her way back.

There were rats down here with her. And secret burial rooms. As in dead people.

Miles and miles of tunnels, some of them undiscovered, Benedek had told her. She wished she could forget.

Benedek.

She'd been an idiot to run off in a huff. She had plenty of time now for his explanation to sink in. Of course, royal marriages would be a matter of state interference. She had known that. She had never planned on marrying the man, for heaven's sake. She hadn't planned on giving him the time of day, to be honest.

She'd resented that she had to fly to Valtria at his bidding. She'd resented him, because she'd thought he would expect her to automatically fall into his bed.

But he had turned out to be a completely different man from her expectations. Smart, brave, gentle. And she did end up in his bed. And that had confused the hell out of her.

She *never* did that. She had studiously kept out of romantic entanglements with opera patrons, no matter how charming or wealthy.

Benedek was different. In hindsight it was obvious that he could be after neither her money nor her fame—he had both in spades. He wanted her. And for the first time in her life the thought of a man wanting her filled her with excitement and a responding need, instead of worry.

She could have beaten her head against the stone wall at the irony. After resenting him from afar for years, in two crazy days she was falling in love with Benedek. The joke was definitely on her. But since the most they were going to find a hundred years from now would be her unidentifiable bones, nobody would be laughing.

She walked resolutely in the direction she thought the palace was, knowing she could be completely wrong and could be walking the opposite way. From time to time, she stopped to call out a single word, "Benedek!"

HE HAD EVERY MAN WHO COULD BE spared from the fight at the palace down in the catacombs. Benedek rushed forward with an industrial strength flashlight.

But as the hours passed, they found nothing.

"Benedek!"

He turned to his brother's voice. "Arpad, what are you doing here?"

"The palace has been taken back. The Army is securing it. The royal guard said you were down here."

"Rayne Williams is lost in the tunnels."

"The fires?"

"All put out. Nothing major."

"Structural damage?" he asked, even knowing that it would take a lot to cause true damage to the three-foot-thick solid stone walls of the palace. Still, he felt relief when Arpad shook his head.

"Rayne Williams's warning made the difference. The rebels didn't have the element of surprise on their side. They weren't able to take up positions before we confronted them." Miklos's voice came from somewhere behind Arpad.

Miklos came into the circle Benedek's flashlight illuminated, watched him for a second, then flashed him a knowing grin. "We'll help you find her," he said.

"Chasing bad guys and hot women, isn't that the Brotherhood's reason for living?" a voice he hadn't been sure he would hear again said. His twin, Lazlo, stepped out of the darkness.

He had a huge bloodstain on his shoulder, haphazardly bandaged. He had his sword in its sheath, a gun in each hand and two ammo belts criss-crossed over his chest. He looked like a bandit. "The bastard got me once, they're not going to get me again."

"What happened at the palace?"

"Some guy named Vilmos was the leader of the attack. He was the captain of the rebel forces, reporting straight to the Freedom

Council," Janos said. "We got this from a rebel we caught and very politely questioned."

Lazlo snorted.

"We tried to find the man, but someone got to him before us. Seems he had an accident with wildlife."

"That was me," Benedek admitted.

Istvan punched his shoulder. "I'm proud of you, little brother."

"What's the plan?" Arpad, as always, was the most focused among them.

"Find Rayne as quickly as we can."

"First to find her gets to have dinner with her?" Lazlo put in. Hard to say whether he was just ribbing his twin or was in earnest. Lazlo was an incorrigible ladies' man. Tabloids loved him. They made money hand over fist covering his exploits. Lazlo didn't know the meaning of low profile. "I'm thinking a midnight carriage ride through the royal arboretum."

"Over my dead body," Benedek said.

"Where are we to look, exactly?" Janos asked, clearly impatient with the twins' spat.

Benedek wished he knew. "Everywhere."

So as they came to an intersection of a

half-dozen tunnels going this way and that, each prince took a handful of royal guards with him and dashed on to save the damsel in distress.

That Lazlo was alive and all his brothers were helping him renewed Benedek's strength. He panned the ground with his flashlight, hoping to spot dainty footprints. He came to another junction. Two tunnels crossed each other. He had to choose between going straight, right, or left. There were two guards with him. They divided up the possibilities among the three of them.

He walked a whole mile forward, finding no sign of her. He did, however, find other signs, carved writing on the floor, written in the secret code of the original Brotherhood of the Crown. Prince Istvan, the anthropologist of the family, was going to have a field day with this. Benedek was so focused on searching for visible clues he almost missed the faint voice in the distance.

"Benedek."

His heart lurched, his lungs filled fully for the first time since she'd walked out on him. "Rayne!" He ran forward as he called her name again.

Then she was there, and the next second in his arms.

"Oh, God. I thought I was going to die here and rats were going to nibble on my bones." She caught herself and buried her face into the crook of his neck. "Sorry."

He was full of relief and some other warm emotion as he said, "You're a performing artist. You're allowed to be a little dramatic."

"I've been that," she said, sounding embarrassed. "Sorry about the brush earlier."

"Don't worry about it. Your passion is one of the things I love about you."

"One?" Her head came up. "There are others?"

He smiled a pure smile of relief. "A couple."

"Like what?" she asked, but then tried to pull back the next second. "Never mind."

He couldn't let her put that distance back between them. "Like this," he said, and kissed her.

He needed her. That was the honest truth. "Were you scared? I came as fast as I could." Hell, he'd been scared. Scared out of his mind for her. He hated to think of her all alone down here.

"Just a little lost."

"I found you now." He brushed his mouth over hers, over and over again, touching, stroking. He needed to stay in constant touch with her as much as possible.

"I'm not scared anymore."

Her lips were sweeter than the sweetest Valtrian honey cake, her curves molded to him. Relief nearly knocked him off his feet. First relief, then desire. He moved them forward until her back met the wall. He explored her mouth, his tongue dancing the most intimate dance with hers, while his free hand slipped under her shirt to her soft skin. It wasn't enough. He set the flashlight on the ground so he could use both hands.

She was warm and willing in his arms, his every fantasy come to life.

"I need you," he confessed. "I should have had enough strength to resist you, but I didn't, and I don't care. I never meant to—"

"I understand protocol," she cut him off, her arms closing around him.

"So you're not mad at me anymore?"

"I won't be your lover once you're married. Not even when you're engaged."

"I wouldn't have—"

"I like you too much to be mad. I need you, too. Whatever the future brings, I want you right now, in this moment and I'm willing to take the risks, I'm willing to let the walls down even if I get hurt."

She humbled him.

Need sang through him and he lifted her the next second, her legs wrapped around his waist. He was fumbling with the zipper on his pants.

She stiffened.

"I'm moving too fast. I'm sorry." He prepared to pull back, even though it was killing him.

"Okay, I do want you, but we can't do this here," she said, sounding shaky. "I almost forgot where we were. I think we're in one of those burial chambers. I have a rule against making love in a cemetery."

For once, she couldn't have been more wrong. He laughed. "Look." He bent for the flashlight and panned the room.

Her eyes went wide. "What is this place?"

"Remember the Brotherhood of the Crown, those hero princes I told you about who lived two hundred years ago?"

She nodded.

"Apparently they were well loved by the ladies. They acquired considerable funds for their cause from feminine donations. The treasure was lost with their death."

"It's here?"

He panned the flashlight over the row of rubies that were set into the stone wall in the ceiling. They formed a strange pattern with a diamond in the middle that sparkled in the flashlight's beam. "Somewhere near."

She turned her wide-eyed gaze to him. "How do you know all this?"

"I saw some hints carved into the rock floor on my way here." Her full mouth was too close to his, too tempting. "So is it all right to make love in a treasure chamber?" He dropped the light.

She closed the distance between their lips. "I don't have any rules against that."

He kissed her thoroughly, stopping only to pull her shirt over her head. He edged her bra straps down her shoulders with his teeth, then kissed her collarbone. "I'm not marrying anyone anytime soon. Spending the last two days with you made me realize how insane that plan had been."

"Did I save you from yourself?" She

placed a soft kiss behind his ear, sending a shot of sharp desire through him.

"You have."

"Oh, good. Then we're even."

"It's not a contest."

"What is it then?"

He bent low enough to take her nipple between his lips. She moaned.

"A slow royal seduction."

"I like that."

He did, too. He turned his full attention to the other nipple. He spoiled it while working to get his pants and underwear down as far as possible. Then he was at her moist opening, then gliding into her tight, wet heat that welcomed him. Her muscles clenched around him, bringing exquisite pleasure.

He began to move inside her.

"We must be breaking a hundred protocols," she said between two sharp pants.

"I've never enjoyed breaking one this much before. I'm rather hoping we'll get to break it over and over again."

He thrust into her sweet, accepting body. He had her at last. And he was never going to let her go.

The thought would have shocked him just

hours ago, but now it seemed natural, the right thing to do, the only sane thing. He had no idea how he was going to break the news to her, or how she was going to react. Pleasure made him forget his worries.

Pleasure built inside him to a level that was nearly unbearable, and then she cried out his name, with enough voice projection to collapse any unstable section of the tunnel. Luckily the ceilings all proved to be steady. His heartbeat was anything but. When he at last spilled his seed deep inside her, all he had strength left for was to control their slow slide to the ground.

She pressed her cheek against his. "I'm glad you found me."

He wasn't sure he could have survived if he hadn't. But before he could tell her that, voices echoed from the distance.

"Rayne?"

"Benedek?"

"There are other people down here?" Rayne jumped off him and grabbed for her clothes.

"Those would be my troublesome brothers."

"What's that?" she pointed to the ground.

And he realized that something had fallen from his pocket.

"Is that my underwear?"

He snatched the sheer piece of fabric.

"Can I have that back?"

"No." He stuffed it into his pocket.

"You—"

"Benedek, is that you there?" Arpad called.

Rayne groaned. "Are they always this intrusive?"

"They're fancying themselves saving us."

"Too late."

He watched as she dressed, her clothes molding to curves that were permanently imprinted on his brain. His heart swelled with emotion.

She was right. His brothers *were* too late.

They'd already saved each other. In more ways than he'd thought possible.

Epilogue

"Fantastic opening," Judi, Miklos's wife, remarked at the royal reception in the palace's grand ballroom, a most adorable little boy in her arm. "I can't believe she stayed all this time to give the performance."

A full month, Benedek thought as he picked up the toy car his nephew had dropped, and handed it back to the child. The kid looked just like Miklos. He tried to picture a little boy who looked like himself, but a dark-haired silver-eyed little girl popped into his mind instead.

"I wonder how many other performances she had to cancel." Judi kissed the top of her son's fuzzy head.

Maybe he was a selfish bastard, but he didn't care. He treasured this last incredibly short month while the opera house had been restored to its full glory, and Rayne and he had been secret lovers.

"You think she'll go back now to the U.S.?" Judi watched him with those sharp eyes of hers that tended to see everything.

"Opening night's over. She has no reason to say." The thought of that about killed him. He'd been in a dark mood for days.

Judi cocked her head. "Then give her one."

He'd thought about that. "A permanent contract at the Valtrian opera?"

Judi rolled her eyes and murmured something about men, then raised a perfectly formed eyebrow and gave him a pointed look.

What?

She couldn't know.

Nobody knew. Rayne and he had been exceedingly discreet.

But maybe he could tell Judi. She was less likely to jump all over him than his brothers.

"The truth is…" He picked his words carefully. "I always admired Rayne. She's an exceptional performer."

Judi cleared her throat.

Okay, fine. "I think when I was younger I might have had some sort of crush on her."

The second eyebrow joined the first. "And it passed?"

His sister-in-law was decidedly grilling him. He didn't like it. But she had other qualities that made him extremely fond of her, and kept Miklos soppy in love with the woman.

"So it passed?" she pushed.

"Not exactly."

"You love her."

He couldn't bring himself to deny it. "Don't tell anyone." He wanted to figure out what to do with it first.

"You're just like your brother." Judi shook her head. "Men are clueless, regardless of breeding and title, you know that?"

"Clueless about what?" he asked before realizing that his question was probably proving her point.

"Everyone pretty much knows already," she said, spelling it out for him.

He froze. "No."

"Oh, yes. Why do you think the Queen spent her entire evening so far talking to her? She loves her, too, by the way. I can tell."

"What are you—"

Judi put her free hand on his shoulder and physically turned him around.

And there was Rayne, laughing with his mother who had been, on occasion, called the Ice Queen. Things looked decidedly less than frosty between them.

That was a relief. But even if it wasn't the case he knew all of a sudden that it wouldn't have mattered. He still couldn't have let her go.

For the last decade he'd carried the guilt of Anna's death and thought the reason it all ended in tragedy was because he'd broken protocol. But in a flash of insight now, he had to wonder if the mistake had been not following his heart. Another realization hit him like a century-old stone wall—Anna was the past, and he needed to let go of that past. Rayne had let down her walls. Now he had to let go of his.

Rayne was his heart. And his future if he was brave enough to claim her.

He would deal with the media, his mother, the chancellor and any number of people who might have objections. The way to make up for Anna's death wasn't to marry a Valtrian debutante without love and make her life miserable.

There was only one thing he could do.

"Would you excuse me? I need to go and make some arrangements."

"Well, hallelujah, praise the Lord, he's seen the light at last." Judi looked pleased as anything. "Keep it simple. She's so in love with you she can barely breathe from it. And don't be trite. Don't call her the music of your life or something like that."

He glared at her.

Her bubbly laughter snuck after him as he turned his back and left.

SHE WAS HAVING A GOOD TIME WITH the Queen, a woman with a mind as sharp and lively as anyone Rayne had ever met. They were talking about how grateful everyone was that the palace hadn't suffered more damage than it had. It was already fully restored to its previous splendor—thanks to Benedek.

"Mother."

Her heart lurched at Benedek's voice behind her. Her body immediately flooded with heat. She wondered if her acute awareness of him whenever he was near would ever pass.

Shouldn't be a problem much longer. Her excuses for staying in the country had officially run out. In a day or two, she'd have to leave. She wrestled down the pain that thought brought to her chest.

The Queen motioned to the chair on her other side. "Sit with us," she told her son. Her face was pale, her voice weak, but she still managed to retain her commanding presence.

Benedek remained standing. "I would like to steal Rayne for a while." He turned to her. "I'd like to show you something outside."

Rayne stood, then curtsied to the Queen. "I need to find my shawl," she told Benedek. "Right there, I think. Let me just get that and I'll be back."

She crossed the room to get to the chair where she'd been sitting earlier. When she got back to the Queen and Benedek, they were deep in conversation, a speculative look coming into the Queen's eyes as she looked her over.

Then the Queen's thin lips stretched into a smile. "I'm looking forward to talking some more with you later."

"Your Highness." She curtsied again before she followed Benedek toward the terrace. "She's so nice. I can't tell you how intimidated I was when a courtier said she wanted to talk to me."

"Intimidated?" Benedek grinned. "She'll

like that. She always complains that she's just a frail old lady now and nobody pays her any mind."

Rayne doubted that, unless the Queen had meant her sons. They were a lively bunch for sure. The Queen deserved a medal for keeping them in line all these years.

Benedek was looking at her funny. "You looked good on stage. I couldn't wait to get you to myself."

"Was the performance all right?" She hadn't seen him since the limo brought her from the opera house to the palace.

"Better than all right. A performance that will be remembered decades from now." He reached for her hand and drew her through the crowd in the reception room.

People were going to notice that. She tried to pull away, self-conscious all of a sudden, but he wouldn't let her.

"Where are we going?"

"To the garden."

She looked outside, into the dark through the windows. "We could talk in here." Right, he was going to show her something. "You can show me tomorrow."

"Trust me on this one?" His gaze sought

hers, warm and heating her further with every nanosecond.

"Any news on the Freedom Council?"

"They suffered a serious blow. It'll take a while before they recover. But that's not what I want to talk to you about. Come."

She stopped stalling and went with him without offering any further resistance. Her reward was a smile that would have made a lesser woman swoon. Even she grew a little weak in the knees. "What's out there?"

"A surprise."

"Better be a good one."

They were at the door to the Queen's private garden, the one she'd seen from above when the palace had been burning. After a month here, she'd gotten to know the place fairly well, although she hadn't gotten around to checking out this particular garden just yet. She wasn't sure if it would be okay. She figured they called it the Queen's *private* garden for a reason.

Two liveried men stood guard at the entrance, in fact.

"Nobody is to come through this door," Benedek told them, then led her down the path, toward the labyrinth in the middle. An eight-foot-tall boxwood hedge made up the labyrinth's walls. It all looked wonderful from above, in daylight. But truth be told, the whole thing wasn't her favorite place in the darkness.

"I'd see it better with sunlight. We could have coffee out here in the morning." She stalled again, talking nonsense. She couldn't imagine anything better than their current routine, drinking coffee in bed together.

"Do you trust me?" He beckoned forward.

"Yes, but it better not be to my detriment."

She drew a deep breath as they entered the maze, which was even darker than the garden around it. He led her with sure steps, without any hesitation, his hand warm around hers.

"And if we get lost?"

"I'll be here with you. But we won't."

Still, concern nudged her. The dark corridors of the labyrinth reminded her of the dark tunnels of the catacombs. "I hope you know what you're doing."

"I've never been more sure." They reached the middle of the labyrinth just as he said that.

A most beautifully appointed gazebo stood in front of them, lit by a thousand candles. It was definitely a fairy-tale moment. The whole place looked enchanted, and she held her breath as she took in every detail.

"What's this?"

"The Queen used to take tea here when she wanted to get away from everyone. She hasn't done it in years. Sometimes I come and read out here."

"It's…" Words defied her.

"You like it?" He sounded urgent, as if her response was especially important to him.

She flashed him an are-you-kidding look before her gaze was drawn back to the magical place before them. Her eyes caught on a champagne bucket and two glasses on the table in the middle of the gazebo. Silk-covered divans edged the gazebo, pushed against the railing.

"Are we celebrating?" She turned back to him.

"That's up to you," he said as he sank to one knee and pulled a velvet box from his pocket.

Her breath caught.

He opened the box.

She stopped breathing altogether. She'd done millions of breathing exercises in her career, but now she couldn't remember a single one of them.

"Remember this?" he asked.

She shook her head, bewildered.

"The diamond in the middle of the ceiling in the treasure chamber you discovered. Istvan had all the stones removed after examining them for any possible clue. They can't be left down there. They'd be hard to guard and he didn't want them to be stolen. My brothers apparently decided to have the rubies made into a tiara for Mother's next birthday. They had the diamond made into a ring and gave it to me. I thought it was because I was the one who found the room. With you," he added.

Her head was spinning. "And that wasn't the reason?"

"They gave it to me because they knew I was in love with you. It was their way of showing support without having to say anything." He grinned. "Even princes are just men. Prefer not to have to express emotion if at all possible. I've been carrying it around in my pocket. I suppose I've been hoping…" He flashed her a disarming, sexy smile.

She was breathing again, but her lung and heart functions were far for normal. "I love your brothers."

"And they love you. Especially Istvan, for

finding the treasure chamber. He just better not love you too much if he wants to live."

"I'm sure he's perfectly capable of finding his own match."

He grinned, then the air grew thick as he took her hand. "Will you marry me, Rayne?"

He couldn't be doing this. Even if she wanted it, wanted him, with all her heart. "What about protocol?"

"Protocol was made to be broken."

"There's an age difference. In a couple of years you might—"

He put a finger over her lips. "I've never loved or wanted anyone half as much as you. You're the one for me. The end."

"The tabloids…"

He scowled. "I'm not even going to respond to that. We'll be too deliriously happy to care."

"You're royalty. I'm a singer."

"Grace Kelly was an actress."

"Your family?"

"Turns out they approve."

"The Queen can't be—"

"As it happens, I mentioned my intentions to her while you went for your shawl. She said she survived two sieges in as many years. She's too tough to be done in by a little scandal."

The gazebo seemed to swirl with her.

"Before I was cross-eyed with love, I used to think all those things mattered," he explained intently. "They don't. Thank God, I had my head straightened out before I lost you. I can't lose you. Rayne?"

A bigger person might have resisted some more, for the good of the crown and all that. She found that she wasn't that noble. "Yes," she said. "Yes!"

He slipped the ring on her finger, a perfect fit, then stood to swing her around in the air. And started kissing her. Then put her down and kept kissing her. Then picked her up all over again to carry her to one of the divans. And kept kissing her.

Then helped her take her clothes off as they kissed some more.

They were naked in the warm night breeze. She was gloriously happy in the arms of her prince who had brought all her walls down and saved her. She kissed him back with heat and passion.

And then they made love as the stars sang above them.

* * * * *

*Celebrate 60 years of pure
reading pleasure with Harlequin®!*

*Harlequin Presents® is proud to introduce
its gripping new miniseries,*
THE ROYAL HOUSE OF KAREDES.
*An exquisite coronation diamond,
split as a symbol of a warring
royal family's feud, is missing!
But whoever reunites the diamond
halves will rule all....*

*Welcome to eight brand-new titles that
unfold to reveal the stories of kings and
queens, princes and princesses torn apart
by pride and power, but finally
reunited by love.*

*Step into the world of Karedes with
BILLIONAIRE PRINCE,
PREGNANT MISTRESS.
Available July 2009
from Harlequin Presents®.*

ALEXANDROS KAREDES, SNOW DUSTING the shoulders of his leather jacket and glittering like jewels in his dark hair, stood at the door. Maria felt the blood drain from her head.

"Good evening, Ms. Santos."

His voice was as she remembered it. Deep. Husky. Perfect English, but with the faintest hint of a Greek accent. And cold, as cold as it had been that awful morning she would never forget, when he'd accused her of horrible things, called her terrible names....

"Aren't you going to ask me in?"

She fought for composure. Last time they'd faced each other, they'd been on his turf. Now they were on hers. She was in command here, and that meant everything.

"There's a sign on the door downstairs,"

she said, her tone every bit as frigid as his. "It says, 'No soliciting or vagrants.'"

His lips drew back in a wolfish grin. "Very amusing."

"What do you want, Prince Alexandros?"

A tight smile eased across his mouth and it killed her that even now, knowing he was a vicious, arrogant man, she couldn't help but notice what a handsome mouth it was. Chiseled. Generous. Beautiful, like the rest of him, which made him living proof that beauty could, indeed, be only skin-deep.

"Such formality, Maria. You were hardly so proper the last time we were together."

She knew his choice of words was deliberate. She felt her face heat; she couldn't help that but she damned well didn't have to let him lure her into a verbal sparring match.

"I'll ask you once more, your highness. What do you want?"

"Ask me in and I'll tell you."

"I have no intention of asking you in. Tell me why you're here or don't. It's your choice, just as it will be my choice to shut the door in your face."

He laughed. It infuriated her but she could hardly blame him. He was tall—six-two, six-three—and though he stood with one shoulder leaning against the door frame, hands tucked casually into the pockets of the jacket, his pose was deceptive. He was strong, with the leanly muscled body of a well-trained athlete.

She remembered his body with painful clarity. The feel of him under her hands. The power of him moving over her. The taste of him on her tongue.

Suddenly, he straightened, his laughter gone. "I have not come this distance to stand in your doorway," he said coldly, "and I am not going to leave until I am ready to do so. I suggest you stand aside and stop behaving like a petulant child."

A petulant child? Was that what he thought? This man who had spent hours making love to her and had then accused her of—of trading her body for profit?

Except it had not been love, it had been sex. And the sooner she got rid of him, the better.

She let go of the doorknob and stepped aside. "You have five minutes."

He strolled past her, bringing cold air and the scent of the night with him. She swung toward him, arms folded. He reached past her, pushed the door closed, then folded his arms, too. She wanted to open the door again but she'd be damned if she was going to get into a who's-in-charge-here argument with him. She was in charge, and he would surely see a tussle over the ground rules as a sign of weakness.

Instead, she looked past him at the big clock above her worktable.

"Ten seconds gone," she said briskly. "You're wasting time, your highness."

"What I have to say will take longer than five minutes."

"Then you'll just have to learn to economize. More than five minutes, I'll call the police."

Instantly, his hand was wrapped around her wrist. He tugged her toward him, his dark-chocolate eyes almost black with anger.

"You do that and I'll tell every tabloid shark I can contact about how Maria Santos tried to buy a five-hundred-thousand-dollar commission by seducing a prince." He smiled thinly. "They'll lap it up."

* * * * *

What will it take for this billionaire prince
to realize he's falling in love
with his mistress…?
Look for
BILLIONAIRE PRINCE,
PREGNANT MISTRESS
by Sandra Marton.
Available July 2009
from Harlequin Presents®.